"There are some things that can't be denied."

Evan went on in the same quiet voice. "It's occurred to me that we're fighting thunder, my dear. Especially after last night's kiss."

Meredith lowered her lashes. "I've already made one bad mistake in my life. This would be another. We don't even like each other. There are things between us that we could never forgive. There are people between us."

"Tell me about one of those people. Tell me about my brother Leigh, Meredith." He looked straight into her eyes.

"It's probably always a terrific gamble to marry for money, Evan," she said quietly.

"If you won't tell me any different, what am I supposed to think?"

"How can I tell you any different?" Meredith asked harshly. "Not you," she whispered.

LINDSAY ARMSTRONG married an accountant from New Zealand and settled down—if you can call it that—in Australia. A coast-to-coast camping trip later, they moved to a six-hundred-acre mixed-grain property, which they eventually abandoned to the mice and leeches and black flies. Then, after a winning career at the track with an untried trotter, purchased "mainly because he had blue eyes," they opted for a more conventional family life with their five children in Brisbane, where Lindsay now writes.

Books by Lindsay Armstrong

HARLEQUIN PRESENTS

559—MELT A FROZEN HEART
607—ENTER MY JUNGLE
806—SAVED FROM SIN
871—FINDING OUT
887—LOVE ME NOT
927—AN ELUSIVE MISTRESS
951—SURRENDER MY HEART
983—STANDING ON THE OUTSIDE

HARLEQUIN ROMANCE

2443—SPITFIRE
2497—MY DEAR INNOCENT
2582—PERHAPS LOVE
2653—DON'T CALL IT LOVE
2785—SOME SAY LOVE
2876—THE HEART OF THE MATTER

LINDSAY ARMSTRONG

the shadow of moonlight

Harlequin Books

TORONTO • NEW YORK • LONDON
AMSTERDAM • PARIS • SYDNEY • HAMBURG
STOCKHOLM • ATHENS • TOKYO • MILAN

Harlequin Presents first edition January 1988
ISBN 0-373-11039-1

Original hardcover edition published in 1987
by Mills & Boon Limited

CHAPTER ONE

MEREDITH SOMMERVILLE pushed her breakfast plate away and reached for the silver coffee-pot. She had breakfasted alone, which was not unusual, but for once a meal that she really enjoyed after having been up before dawn had been remarkably tasteless. Not that the fluffy cheese omelette could be blamed. Like everything else at Sommerville—bar herself, she thought with a grimace—it had been perfect. No, the problem was a severe case of abstraction and the feeling that she had the Sword of Damocles hanging over her head, to put it mildly.

She sighed and sipped her coffee and gazed absently at her unflattering reflection in the coffee-pot. She was a fairly tall girl, on the thin side for her height but still, at twenty-two, giving glimpses of what at nineteen had been an almost perfect figure, although she sometimes walked with a very slight limp now. Her hair was dark gold and she wore it at shoulder length in a smooth pageboy style. Her eyebrows were slightly darker than her hair and framed light hazel eyes with flecks of green in them, and her skin was smooth too and lightly tanned.

But as she sat sipping her coffee, her thoughts were not on her looks at all. Instead, she was remembering what a magical dawn it had been on the Upper Hunter, with streaks of rose-pink and pale yellow gradually fading from the sky as she had cantered Nuriootpa through the brood mare paddocks, checking on all the mums, most of which had leggy foals frisking at foot.

And on the way back to the stables, the high, clear blue

sky had been a perfect foil for the white walls and gables of the old winery—a unique example of Cape Dutch architecture in faraway Australia and the whim of an earlier Sommerville, perhaps conscious of his trace of Huguenot ancestry, who had gone to South Africa to study wine-making.

Not that any wine had been made at Sommerville for a long time, in fact horses were its mainstay, although grapes were still grown to be sold to other wine-makers. Nor was Sommerville the only establishment in the Upper Hunter to have experienced futility in the matter of producing vintages not to be scorned by the Lower Hunter Valley— virtually next door, in a manner of speaking, and the oldest wine-producing area in Australia—and also the most élitist, according to some. Although nowadays there *were* some good wines coming from the Upper Hunter.

But if the Sommerville family had failed at wine-making it had succeeded at just about everything else the Hunter Valley region of New South Wales had to offer, particularly coal. And not only the mining of it; they had spread their empire through to related industries such as haulage and shipping.

And at the heart of this empire, although various members of the family came and went, or stayed away, was Sommerville itself with its unique winery that stood idle, its sprawling, magnificent old homestead, its position on the beautiful tablelands around Scone which were renowned for the breeding of racehorses, and its stud, the reputation of which reached into most corners of the thoroughbred industry.

It sometimes gave Meredith a spurious sense of satisfaction to know that she shared a very small part of that reputation. Sommerville stood three stallions, but it was not that side of the business that interested her. Nor was she much into bloodlines, a never-flagging source of conversation amongst the stud employees. It was the mares that interested her and fascinated her, and she had gradually, without quite knowing how, apart from her observation of them, become fairly adept at being able to judge when a mare was due to drop her foal or to get into difficulties foaling. Enough of a judge at least to have acquired a reputation of her own, so that the remark—'Mrs Meredith was right again'—when a mare foaled to her prediction, was fairly commonly heard amongst the stud staff.

Yet on that chilly but sparkling autumn morning, Meredith was contemplating leaving Sommerville.

The sound of footsteps disturbed her reverie and she glanced up and stiffened as a tall, fair man walked into the breakfast-room.

'Meredith,' Evan Sommerville said briefly, by way of greeting, and strode over to the sideboard.

Meredith's knuckles whitened round her cup before she put it down quietly and stood up and started to walk out.

But he said her name again, sharply, and she swung back hesitantly.

Evan Sommerville was in his middle thirties, over six foot tall, and his fair hair was thick and that moment damp and darker-looking than normal, and bearing the marks of a comb.

He also possessed a pair of rather hard grey eyes and an aquiline nose, set in a strong, squarish face. All of which, when added to his well proportioned body, gave him an air of arrogance, impatience and strength. But it wasn't only an air—he was frequently arrogant and impatient. And even dressed as he was now, in a pair of faded working jeans and a dark-blue sweater with leather elbow patches, that was fraying around one wrist, he was intensely, dominatingly and, according to many, irresistibly masculine.

They stared at each other, he with a plate in one hand and Meredith standing defensively beside her chair.

Until he remarked, 'I don't see why we shouldn't observe the bare minimum of civility.'

A spark of anger lit Meredith's hazel eyes, but she lowered her lashes immediately, and said to the back of the chair, 'Good morning, Evan.'

'Good morning, Merry,' he drawled, and smiled as she flinched visibly. 'Sit down,' he went on as he turned back and dished himself up sausages and a poached egg. 'Have a cup of coffee with me.' He sat down himself and unfurled a linen napkin.

'I've just finished.'

'Then have another,' he interrupted. 'And you might pour me one, if it's not too much of an imposition.'

Meredith gritted her teeth but sat down obediently and poured two cups, for which effort she received another cool, taunting smile. And he said, 'I gather passive resistance is to be the order of the day today, Merry.'

She bent her head and her heavy hair fell forward. 'Have I ever offered any other kind?' she murmured, glancing at him obliquely.

He gazed at her with an expression of curious irony in his grey eyes until she looked away. He said then, 'But you do have a habit of looking at me with deadly intent sometimes.'

'I'm surprised you've even noticed,' she retorted.

'Ah, but I've always noticed a great deal about you, my dear Meredith,' he replied, and quite dispassionately subjected her to a leisurely scrutiny that brought a flush to her cheeks, which deepened as he added, 'There's one thing I've never denied about you. You're very lovely in your own quiet way.'

She closed her eyes and willed herself to stay calm, and

said very quietly, 'Don't expect me to thank you for that.'

He shrugged and grinned. 'I didn't, actually. I suppose you've been up and about for hours?'

'Yes.'

'Not only lovely but so industrious! I'm sure we Sommervilles had no idea what a valuable member of the family you were to become,' he remarked, but his eyes mocked her in a way she knew all too well.

'Evan . . .' She took a steadying breath. 'Evan, if you've got something to say to me, please say it. Do you want me to leave now that you've come back to live here? Well, I've already decided to.'

Evan Sommerville stopped eating and his mouth hardened. 'Oh no, you haven't,' he said grimly. 'It's only an extension of that hard-done-by, poor-little-widow act you do so well and particularly for the benefit of my beloved grandmother. But the truth of the matter is that you've really dug yourself in here, haven't you, Meredith? Like the gold-digger you are at heart.'

They stared at each other, Meredith suddenly pale and with her lips trembling. But she hadn't cried for a long time and she had no intention of giving Evan Sommerville that satisfaction.

'Then you'll just have to wait and see, won't you?' she whispered—and stood up purposefully.

He stood up too and politely helped her with her chair. 'I'll do that, Merry,' he said. 'But there's an old saying about wishes and horses, isn't there?'

For a moment she was tempted, really tempted, to hit him. But sanity prevailed almost as soon as the thought crossed her mind, and she shivered inwardly at her incredible flash of temerity, wondering briefly how he would have reacted—which caused her to back away a step and stumble.

He put out a lean, tanned hand and took her elbow to steady her. 'Of course there's the other saying,' he drawled with that attractive, lazy smile that she mistrusted so devoutly. 'The one about—if looks could kill?'

'Oh,' she said huskily, 'I lost faith in that one ages ago— not long after I met you, in fact. But as you so rightly surmised earlier, it's a habit I find hard to break.'

'Funnily enough, it's about the only habit of yours I admire, Meredith. At least it's honest.'

'Well, in that case,' she said through her teeth, 'the next time I *honestly* feel like hitting you, I do hope you won't take exception to it!' And she glared up at him.

He narrowed his grey eyes and said softly, 'You could certainly experiment if you care to, Merry. But I think you made the right decision just now. It mightn't be a good idea. So there will be a next time?' he added coolly, and released her elbow.

Meredith breathed distraughtly, then took the only course left open to her. She walked out on Evan Sommerville, to hear him laughing quietly behind her.

An hour later, she raised her flushed face from her pillow where she'd buried it in an agony of remorse and anger. But her hazel eyes were still dry although bitter as she looked around the lovely, old-fashioned but comfortable Wedgwood blue and cream bedroom that had been hers for over two years. And she began to plan.

'You're very quiet, Meredith.'

Meredith looked up and smiled in the lamplight. 'Am I, Mrs Sommerville? I hadn't realised.'

She and Evan's grandmother were sitting in front of a huge log fire in the drawing-room, pursuing their separate occupations, which in Mrs Sommerville's case was a game of patience, and in Meredith's, a crossword puzzle.

'I do hope,' Mrs Sommerville said, and paused to put a red jack on a black queen, 'I do hope this latest decision of Evan's has nothing to do with it?' She looked up suddenly and across at Meredith out of grey eyes that were remarkably similar to her grandson's.

In fact there was a lot of Evan's grandmother in Evan Sommerville, Meredith had often thought. Which probably accounted for the occasionally abrasive nature of their relationship, despite the affection and esteem they really held each other in. But in Mrs Sommerville, although she could be positively regal from the top of her snowy white bun to the tips of her toes, and was possessed of a spirit of indomitability, those qualities were tempered by kindness and wisdom.

'Meredith?'

'Oh.' Meredith put down her crossword. 'No.'

'My dear, it's always been quite obvious to me that you and Evan rub each other up the wrong way.'

Meredith was silent, staring into the flames.

'But you do have as much right to be here as he does.'

She looked across at Mrs Sommerville's lined, patrician face at last. 'I can't tell you how much I appreciate you saying that, but ...'

'It's only the truth,' Mrs Sommerville broke in. 'You know,' she added slowly, 'I must say this decision of Evan's has surprised me. In fact I did wonder if he was thinking of settling down and taking a wife.' She rolled her eyes impishly at Meredith.

Meredith opened her mouth, then closed it, and said instead, 'He's always been very fond of Sommerville, though, hasn't he?'

'That's true,' Mrs Sommerville conceded. 'I do think that he's always cared about it more than either of his brothers   but then Leigh was the kind of person who was never happy in one place for long, which you as his wife must have known.' She was silent for a moment and a shadow crossed her face. 'I always felt it was a pity that Leigh and Evan . . . fell out so often, you know, and I often think it wasn't so much either of their faults, as circumstances. When their parents died, Leigh was still at school and Evan was the one who had to shoulder a really . . . rather vast amount of responsibility,' she said thoughtfully. 'Which he did very well. But there's no doubt Leigh's attitude annoyed him. Yet all Leigh wanted to do was the one thing he was really good at. But I do think basically there was a bond between them, don't you, Meredith?'

'Yes.'

'As for Christian——' Mrs Sommerville smiled suddenly, 'but I don't have to tell you about him, do I? And that's the other thing! Do you know that Evan is handing over to Chris? Well, he is. He said to me he thought it was time at last Chris learnt to shoulder some of the responsibility, which might be true, but I just,' she cast Meredith a comical look, 'shudder slightly to think about that!'

Meredith had to smile herself.

'Of course Evan will be able to keep a hand on the reins from up here. It's not as it we're up on the moon. But all the same,' Mrs Sommerville stared into the fire, 'well, I'm a little surprised at Evan's decision. I thought he,' she shrugged, 'enjoyed big business.'

'Perhaps he just feels as if he needs a break?' Meredith suggested.

Mrs Sommerville transferred her gaze down to the cards in her hands and then deliberately shuffled them. 'Perhaps . . .'

'That's cheating,' said Meredith with a grin.

'I do cheat sometimes,' Mrs Sommerville confessed. 'But

to get back to what all started this. You're not only quiet but you're looking a little drawn, Meredith, I've noticed. Is your leg . . .?'

'No,' Meredith interrupted hastily. 'It's fine.'

'Then you must need a break. Go down to Sydney for a while—after all, why not? You've certainly earned it, and lovely as Sommerville is, even I get a hankering for the bright lights occasionally.'

'I . . .' Meredith looked away and bit her lip. For ever since her disastrous conversation with Evan that very morning, she'd been steeling herself to bring up just this suggestion, and here it was being handed to her on a platter. 'I . . .' Oh God, what to *tell* her, though? 'I might just do that. Now that Evan's here with you,' she added lamely.

'He's not here quite yet. He's gone to spend a few days with the Healeys at Pokolbin—do you know them?'

'No, I don't think so. Do you mean the Healeys of Wattavale Winery?'

'Yes, those famous Healeys,' Mrs Sommerville said with a grin. 'Which, incidentally, is what started me thinking about wives. Sarah Healey is back from overseas. She and Evan were quite taken with each other once, I believe. I have never,' she wrinkled her brow, 'been quite able to visualise what kind of a wife Evan would choose, though, you know, Meredith.'

'Doesn't . . . Sarah Healey fit the bill?'

'I don't know. That's the problem. I mean, she's nice enough, in fact she's *very* nice and rather bright and I've known her since she was a baby. I have nothing whatever against her! Perhaps the problem is that I suspect Evan . . . would be rather a hard man to please.'

'Oh?'

'Well, yes. I think he's a very sophisticated, complex man

and also that he's had—in a manner of speaking—the pick of the crop at his feet for quite some years. And discarded many of them,' she said ruefully. 'Which is not to say,' she added slowly, 'that that kind of a man couldn't one day fall deeply in love although he might not altogether . . . relish it. But anyway,' she went on with sudden vigour and a wave of her cards, 'I have enough people to fuss over me as if I were in my dotage without having to have you or Evan on hand constantly. And Chris said he would be popping up in the next few days. God knows, but I can't help finding that boy amusing for all that I suspect he's as mad as a March hare. No, you do it, Meredith, and don't stop to think about it! And I shall look forward to seeing you back in full bloom!'

Having given in to Mrs Sommerville's determination to book her into the Sydney Hilton, Meredith left Sommerville the next day, spent one night there then cancelled her reservation and indicated that she'd changed her plans. And she drove steadily north out of Sydney, the way she'd come, until Newcastle, but instead of heading inland for Scone there, she kept heading north up the Pacific Highway.

Several days of easy driving brought her to Ballina where she chose a motel right on the Richmond River. They gave her an upstairs room, and she gasped as she entered it. For the sun was setting on the broad reach of the river below, and a wide, corner window gave a marvellous view upstream and down. She stared out at the liquid sheet of colour, at the pelicans, at the distant bank cloaked in a haze of silvery-green mangroves, at a stark silver and black tree-trunk sticking up out of the water upon which a lone ibis was resting, and knew immediately that she would stay in Ballina for longer than the one night she had planned on.

She slept a lot for the first couple of days and, between times, spent hours sitting at the table at the corner window, watching the river in all lights, and trying to come to terms with what she had done—trying to square her conscience with having left Sommerville like a thief in the night, for all that she had departed in broad daylight. But with the express intention of never returning, she kept reminding herself. Should I have told her? But what good would that have done? No, better this way, surely. And she was wrong, Mrs Sommerville, I didn't have as much right to be there as Evan. I probably had none at all.

Then she began to do some sightseeing.

Ballina was not big and most mornings or evenings a fishing fleet set out to sea from the mouth of the Richmond River. But apart from the fascination of the river, on the other side of town was the surf of the Pacific. It was too cold to swim in that surf, but she walked along the beach frequently, listening to and watching the waves pounding.

One day she took the road north to Byron Bay, only a half-hour drive but along a magnificent coastline. And she stopped and made herself climb the smooth turf of Lennox Head and later drove up the tortuous road to the Byron Bay lighthouse atop Cape Byron, to stand gasping in the wind and awed, on the most easterly point of Australia.

The cape rose from a rocky base up steep, wooded slopes to a narrow ridge down which you could walk from the lighthouse to the tip—if you were game enough. Meredith was not. In fact she found gazing out over the vast wrinkled ocean from that height quite amazing enough, and a little eerie.

It was two days after her visit to Cape Byron and eight days after she'd left Sommerville that she drove up to the charming village of Alstonville for lunch. On the way back, latish in the afternoon, it started to rain torrentially and just the short walk from her car to her room got her drenched. So she took a shower because she was cold as well as soaked, and wrapped her hair in a fluffy white towel and pulled on a thick, jade-green towelling robe that belted around her waist.

Then she made herself a cup of tea and took it over to the window, to see that the fierce squall had passed and that the river was reflecting the pale, bright grey of the sky as a fishing boat nosed its way upstream with an attendant cloud of brilliant white seagulls diving about it for scraps.

'Rather them than me out in that,' she murmured. 'I much prefer solid ground anyway.'

It was then that she noticed a white envelope on the carpet in front of the door and realised she must have missed it when she had dashed in. But despite a nameless feeling of apprehension that gripped her suddenly, all the note requested was that she contact Reception when she came in.

She frowned and poured her tea, wondering why they should want her, because she had booked her room for a fortnight.

But all of a sudden, she found that feeling of apprehension growing into something more, something like panic—a feeling that she knew well—although why a simple note should have triggered it, she couldn't say, only acknowledge that she hadn't been as successful as she had thought in burying Sommerville in her subsconscious. Why can't I just forget it all? she asked herself anguishedly. Why do I feel as if there's something pulling me back—I vowed I would never go back, but . . .

She took a deep breath and forced herself to calm down and stared confusedly at the note once more.

Oh well, she thought then, only one way to find out about it, and she picked up the phone, but put it down again as a knock sounded on the door.

And when she opened it, the ground was no longer so solid beneath her feet, because Evan Sommerville stood outside on the small landing.

Meredith's mouth fell open, and unwittingly one hand crept up to clutch at the neck of her robe. 'Y-you!' she whispered, going pale. 'How did you find me?'

His mouth twisted and his grey eyes were sardonic. 'I had to have a police message broadcast. The motel people here heard it, but you weren't in.'

'A ... a police message?' she stammered. 'Are you charging me ...' Her hazel eyes dilated and her knees started to give way.

'Meredith,' he said imperatively, then he swore and picked her up, carrying her into the room, where he put her down in a chair. 'Of course I'm not charging you with anything! What the hell gave you that idea?'

She stared up at him with her eyes still huge and dark in the pallor of her face.

'Don't look like that,' he said impatiently, and picked up one of her hands to massage it. Then he noticed her cup of tea and said, 'Drink some of this. I don't suppose you've got anything stronger?'

'No.'

'Finish it, then.'

She did, and some colour came back to her cheeks.

'I don't understand,' she said eventually, with her hands to her brow.

'That's obvious,' he replied ironically, straightening to put the cup down and push his hands irritably into his trouser pockets.

'Well,' Meredith said helplessly, 'you have accused me of

being an impostor and a fraud from time to time.'

'Not as an indictable offence.'

'Then why the police?' Her hazel eyes were confused and a little frightened again.

He stared at her. 'I'm sorry,' he said abruptly, then, 'I didn't mean to scare the living daylights out of you. It was an emergency police message.'

Meredith's lips parted and a look of comprehension dawned. 'Not Mrs Sommerville?' she whispered.

He nodded. 'She fell down and broke her hip, and the shock of it brought on pneumonia. She's been very ill—still is. And on top of it, whenever she's lucid, she keeps asking for you, urgently.'

Meredith swallowed.

Evan went on a little wearily, 'Unfortunately, or perhaps fortunately now that I've found you, I don't think it's dawned on her that you . . . left for good, Meredith. Or am I wrong?' he asked very quietly, his grey eyes never wavering from her stricken hazel ones.

Meredith pressed her hands together. 'It's what you wanted me to do,' she said huskily.

'Perhaps. I never thought you'd do it, though.'

'That was all the more reason why I had to do it.'

'But,' he paused and searched her oval face, 'not to tell her anything?'

Tears, genuine tears pricked Meredith's eyelids, but she battled against them and won, although her eyes were suspiciously bright as she said, barely audibly, 'Tell her what? That in your eyes I'm an adulterous gold-digger? That it's impossible for you and me to live under the same roof? I'm sorry, Evan, but I just couldn't do it. She would have insisted on having it all out. I,' her voice cracked a little, 'thought it would be best for *you* to tell her—after I'd gone.'

He was silent, and after a time turned his head to stare out of the window.

'Is she ... she's not going to die, is she?'

He looked back at her at last. 'Not if I can help it. But,' he sat down suddenly opposite Meredith, 'she's not young and ...'

He stopped for a moment and his eyes were stark. Then he squared his shoulders as if they were stiff and cramped. 'Meredith, I'll do a deal with you. If you come back with me now, I'll put the past behind us. Not to be mentioned again so that we *can* live under the same roof. Anyway, no,' he lifted a hand to check her, 'it *is* past and better forgotten. Leigh's been dead for over two years now and I've—well, I've been pretty brutal sometimes. More ... than was necessary. I'm sorry.'

'Evan ...' Meredith stared at him, shock and confusion registering in her expression.

'You're right,' he said drily. 'You suspect me of having an ulterior motive. But you're very fond of her too, aren't you?'

'*Yes*, but ...'

'Meredith, she took you in and she's treated you like a daughter. And not only because she has an almost biblical sense of family and saw it as her duty, especially when you were so ill after the accident. But also because she's grown to love you as a daughter or a granddaughter. The shock of your leaving on top of what's happened to her wouldn't be a ... great way to repay her, would it?'

'It might never have been too easy for her, Evan.'

Their glances caught and held.

'No,' he said finally. 'My error.'

'I ...' Meredith took a breath and put a rather shaky hand to her head, to discover that she still had a now very damp towel around it. She unwound it dazedly and ran her fingers through her hair, pushing the damp dark gold strands behind her ears. Then she said hesitatingly, 'It could only ever be ... such a sham, though, couldn't it?'

He said, 'We might surprise ourselves.'

In the last of the daylight, her hazel eyes seemed to have absorbed the jade-green of her robe as she looked at him. 'I doubt that, Evan.'

His eyes hardened. 'Then perhaps we can make it a convincing enough sham for a very sick old lady who is very dear to both of us. After all, we haven't been exactly strangers over the past three years. I've spent time at Sommerville. We've ... managed, you and I.'

'Oh yes,' said Meredith. 'Yes. Not that we've fooled her completely. She told me once she could see that we rub each other up the wrong way. Her words.'

A faint spark of humour lit his grey eyes. 'And what did you reply to that, I'm sure unwittingly incongruous statement, my dear Meredith?' he drawled.

'Nothing,' she said barely audibly, and after a moment deliberately unclenched her hands. 'All right, I'll come. But on one condition, Evan. That as soon as she's well enough, I can begin to make plans to lead my own life. I don't mean to desert her entirely, but—well, it's not such an unnatural thing to want to do. In fact I've mentioned it to her a few times but she ...' She shrugged.

'Wouldn't hear of it?' he suggested.

'No. She didn't seem to think I was capable of it.' Meredith's voice was faintly wry.

'Are you?'

'Physically, quite capable. And there must be other fortunes to seek,' she murmured.

Again their glances clashed.

'You're not exactly penniless now,' he said.

'No, I'm not. Thanks to Leigh.'

'On the other hand, you've barely touched what he left you, have you?'

'Perhaps I'm saving it for a rainy day.' She smiled for the first time, a faint, cool curve of her lips. 'How did you get here?'

He didn't answer immediately. Then he got up abruptly and switched on the light. 'I flew up. Unfortunately I haven't been able to organise a flight back tonight, so I thought we might drive your car down.'

Meredith turned her head from the window to look at him. 'You were very sure of me, weren't you, Evan?'

'Yes. Does that upset you?'

Meredith contemplated him silently for a time. Then she closed her eyes briefly. 'Yes, unfortunately. Because I'd do anything for your grandmother.'

'That's what I was trying to suggest earlier,' he said with irony. 'That her well-being is something bigger than our differences.'

She got up herself. 'It won't take me long to pack.'

CHAPTER TWO

'I'VE GOT two brothers, Merry, one older and one younger—Evan and Christian, in that order.'

'What are they like?'

'Evan is very much the head of the family and Chris—well, is just Chris.'

'You don't seem to be a very close family, Leigh.'

'I guess we're not, Merry—to the despair of our grandmother.'

'Why is that?' Meredith had asked.

'For one thing, Evan tends to treat *me* . . . well, let's just say big brother doesn't altogether approve of my lifestyle.'

'Are they married?'

'Evan and Christian? No—not to my knowledge.'

'Do they know you are now, Leigh?'

'Not yet. But you'll get to meet them in due course, my sweet. Why are you so worried about it?'

'I'm not,' Meredith replied slowly and not entirely truthfully. 'I just think it's a bit strange.' And it occurred to her that she had left it a bit late to be bothered about Leigh's total disinclination to inform his family that he had married her.

Over three years later, as she sat beside Evan as they drove swiftly through the night, the thought returned to plague her. I must have been mad, she mused, and moved restlessly.

Evan turned his head towards her. 'What's the matter?'

'Nothing.'

'Why don't you try to sleep? You could hop into the back.'

'No, I'm all right.'

They had had a quick meal before leaving Ballina but had caught up with the rain-squall within an hour, which had slowed them considerably. Now, though, the night was clear and starry and Evan was taking full advantage of it, sending the car through the silvery night at speed.

Meredith found this nerve-racking to say the least, but he drove with such confidence that she said nothing. And finally she had found herself relaxing and thinking of other things. The past, mainly. And not long after he had suggested she try to sleep, she did fall into a half-dozing state but with it still all on her mind . . .

'Leigh—Leigh, don't. You mustn't!'

'Mustn't what, Merry?'

'Do what you're doing. *No!*'

'I can guarantee you'll like it.'

'But,' her voice had been shaken and breathless as she had tried to do up the buttons of her blouse, 'we're not married or anything like that.'

'Are you asking me to marry you, Merry?'

'No! I mean—of course not. Leigh, *please!*'

He had lifted his head and she had stared up at him shocked and a little frantic until he had laughed softly and kissed the tip of her nose. 'Relax, baby. You really are one, aren't you?'

'I'm nineteen.'

'And a virgin to boot!'

'Well, yes. Is there anything wrong in that?' she had asked defensively.

'*Au contraire!* It's exactly—it's one of the things I love about you. Together with that soft pale skin, scared greeny eyes, lovely figure . . . All right, let's do it.'

'Do what?'

'Let's get married, my darling Merry, what else?'

She had gasped and gone quite pale.

'Now what's wrong?' he drawled. 'I thought . . .'

'Leigh,' she had interrupted tearfully, 'don't tease me.'

'But I'm not!'

'We . . . we don't know each other very well,' she had stammered.

'It's been nearly three months now, Merry.'

She had opened her mouth but shut it again in confusion. For it had been nearly three months since Leigh Sommerville had walked into her life and certainly dominated her thoughts almost to the exclusion of everything else. It had happened, of all places, at the Royal Easter Show. A friend Meredith worked with had persuaded her to go on the Easter Monday, but had soon discovered that the only thing that had riveted Meredith's attention was the show-jumping events being held in the main arena. And they had finally come to a laughing arrangement that Meredith should watch the horses to her heart's content, and that they would meet up later in the afternoon.

And midway through the day, Meredith had found herself drawn as if by a magnet to the area where the horses were, behind the arena. And she had been stroking the velvety nose of a grey mare tied up to a float when a shadow had fallen across her and she had looked up to see a tall man in white jodhpurs, black boots and white shirt and tie, watching her.

She had blushed and started to back away embarrassedly

when he had said, 'Don't go. You look as if you were enjoying that.'

'I was. I love horses,' she had said shyly. 'Is she yours?'

'Uh-huh.'

'I haven't seen her in the ring. She's lovely.'

'Her turn's coming. You're rather lovely yourself.'

Meredith had coloured again and looked down at her simple attire—a pair of jeans and a daffodil-yellow sweater.

'My guess is you would look good in a sack,' the tall stranger had said softly, and smiled at her engagingly. 'Am I being very forward?' he had enquired then. 'Sorry, let's go back to the beginning. I'm Leigh Sommerville. How do you do?'

'How do you do?' she had murmured. 'I'm Meredith Conway. Oh!'

'What?'

'I've just realised who you are. I mean, I saw you jumping this morning, but I didn't recognise you without your hat. You're very good.'

'I do seem to be having one of my better days,' he had replied with a glint of laughter in his blue eyes. 'Do you know what would top it off?'

'A—perfect round on this mare?' she had hazarded.

'Well, that too,' he had conceded. 'But let's not go asking for miracles. No, I meant if you would agree to have dinner with me tonight.'

Meredith had hesitated. She had only been in Sydney for six months and was still a little wary of the pitfalls of big city life.

But Leigh Sommerville had added persuasively, 'Tell you what, let me earn it. Say you'll come if I do have a perfect round on Nuriootpa.' He had indicated the mare.

She had had to laugh. 'And if you don't?'

'But I will—with that as an incentive.'

'All right,' she had agreed a little breathlessly.

Nor had she reneged when she had discovered, from listening to the annnouncer's comments introducing Leigh Sommerville on Nuriootpa, that the mare was a champion show-jumper of the highest calibre, as indeed she proved in a faultless round. Although over dinner she had suggested that Nuriootpa hadn't seemed to need any incentive at all.

'Oh, she can have her off days,' he had murmured, but with a wicked little smile.

And considering how shy Meredith was, the evening had been a great success. She had found herself telling Leigh Sommerville about her childhood in the Blue Mountains hamlet of Kurrajong, of her passion for horses from an early age, even about her family—or lack of it. Her father had been the local doctor and something of an institution in the area until his death five years earlier. She had been unaware of the pain in her eyes as she had spoken of her gentle, scholarly father who had also been her best friend.

'What about your mother?'

'She died when I was a baby. I don't think he ever got over it, and he was a lot older than she was.'

'What happened then?'

'I went to live with my aunt—his sister.'

'Not a great success,' Leigh had suggested.

'No. Well—how did you guess?' she had asked.

'You have the most expressive eyes.'

Meredith had grimaced, and said unhappily, 'They've given a false impression this time. They were very good to me, my aunt and uncle, really. But they have six children of their own, you see . . . Besides, I missed my father so much.' She had stared past Leigh Sommerville for a time, thinking of her aunt's noisy, erratic and cramped household that had been so unlike her own home and upbringing, of the constant fights between children—and parents for that matter—of the consciousness that she just didn't fit in, of the fact that she had had to part with her beloved pony too.

'So you came to the big smoke, Meredith?'

She had blinked and said hastily, 'Yes, I was very lucky to get the first job I applied for here. Otherwise I'd be in New Zealand now with them. My uncle was a Kiwi and he got this bee in his bonnet about going back, so he uprooted them all. They wanted me to go with them, but I put my foot down for once. My aunt writes to me every week, though, and gets into a panic if I don't write back immediately.'

'What kind of job have you got?'

'Bank clerk. It's a good job,' she had added.

'But not the stuff dreams are made of?'

She had grinned wryly. 'No. But it's well paid, and anyway, my aunt thinks if you get into a bank, you're set for life. My getting this job was one thing that made her feel happier about leaving me. Getting into the Y.W.C.A. was another.'

'And how do you like Sydney?'

She had hesitated.

'You don't?'

'Yes, I do!'

'But you get lonely,' Leigh Sommerville had said quietly.

'Sometimes,' she had confessed.

Loneliness hadn't been a problem from then on, though. For Leigh Sommerville had made it obvious that he was very attracted to her, had been from the moment he had laid eyes on her, stroking Nuriootpa's nose, he had claimed, and for her part, though slower to be fired, the attraction had been shared. She had liked his tall, fair good looks, his teasing sense of humour, his undoubted *savoir-faire*, and it had been impossible not to be flattered by his interest. While not ever having heard of the Sommervilles, she had realised very soon that Leigh came from a wealthy family—his lifestyle and his horses gave clear indication of it, although he rarely mentioned his background. But mingled with the flattery had been a trace of wariness in Meredith's mind.

He was, she had kept reminding herself, a twenty-seven-year-old playboy—well, yes, that might sound unkind, but was it inaccurate? He certainly didn't have to work for a living and what he spent most of his time doing, show-jumping, although it was arduous and gruelling to have reached the heights he had, was also a very expensive pastime.

Whereas she was a nineteen-year-old nobody.

Only, as if he had read her mind, Leigh had been very circumspect during those first weeks. But finally he had started to kiss her and hold her and she had found herself responding and with increasing desire—up to a point. But it had also become harder to observe that point.

Then he had asked her to marry him, at first taking her breath away, but he had been insistent, and while she had hesitated another month, he had laid skilful siege to her already flimsy defences.

But he does want to marry me, she had kept telling herself. That's got to mean he loves me. As for *me*—well, I don't know how much longer I can hold out, or whether I want to.

She had married him one spring morning nearly four months after the Royal Easter Show, and been blissfully happy for the next three months despite her aunt's agonised

letters which had claimed she was too young to be
marrying anyone, too young to know her own mind.
Meredith had obscurely pondered these things too, and
been obscurely comforted by the fact that her aunt had
delayed marrying until she was twenty-five. For although
she had stuck to her husband and borne him six children,
she sometimes appeared to regret the day she had laid eyes
on him.

Nor had Meredith's happiness evaporated overnight
after three months. In fact it had been a gradual process
which had seen their marriage finally grind to a painful
halt. But the seeds had been there perhaps from the
beginning, starting with their very different characters.

Leigh had a quixotic, gypsy streak in him that had
sometimes alarmed her even during those first three
months. But her lifestyle had changed so dramatically and
glamorously she had put it down partly to that, and closed
her mind to those vague fears. Not hard to do when it was
obvious her slender, curved body afforded Leigh a great
deal of pleasure and when she appeared to be the very
centre of his life. Only it had slowly dawned on her that
although it was exciting and glamorous following the show-
jumping circuit which brought her into contact with horses
again, which she loved, it was a life without roots, and she
became conscious of a desire to settle somewhere, to have
their own home rather than a series of luxurious hotels and
apartments, to have a baby.

But when she had mentioned children to Leigh once he
had said, 'I prefer you the way you are, Merry. Definitely.'

'But you don't mean—not ever?'

'Darling, have you seen any pregnant ladies lately?'

'Yes—no, I mean . . . Leigh,' she had said helplessly.

'Aren't you happy with me?'

'You know I am.'

'Then stop worrying about *Kinder, Kirche und Küche*, sweetheart, and come and show me how much you love me.'

She'd done just that, warmly and tenderly, but even so had not quite been able to still the feeling of fear in her heart.

By the time they had been married for eight months, that feeling had grown to panic, because it had become increasingly obvious that Leigh was tiring of her.

Meredith stirred restlessly, feeling the leather of the car seat beneath her cheek, not knowing that she had fallen into an uneasy doze while she had been remembering, not knowing what had woken her from it, not knowing where she was. Only that she was cramped and cold.

She sat up abruptly and as she did so, out of the darkness a huge pair of lights was bearing down on them together with a sound like a low rumble of thunder.

And she opened her mouth and screamed and cowered frantically into her seat as the huge semi-trailer roared past them, and Evan brought the car to a jarring halt on the side of the road.

'My God, Meredith, you could have ... *Meredith*!'

But she was weeping hysterically now and shaking so that her teeth were chattering and a film of cold sweat gleamed on her brow.

He stared at her with his lips parted, then his eyes narrowed and he frowned, and reached across to pull her into his arms. 'All right, it's all right. I understand.'

But it was a long time before she was able to calm down. And even then she could only talk jerkily and with difficulty and the occasional tremor still racked her body. 'I thought . . . it was happening again. No, that I was back there with . . . and . . . Leigh . . . Oh God, will I ever forget!'

'Don't,' he said gently.

'I can't help it. I . . . I never drive at night.'

'You should have *told* me.'

'No. I mean it's important to get there as soon as possible. And if I hadn't fallen asleep . . .'

'It's important to get you there not looking a nervous wreck,' he said evenly. 'We'll stop at the next town and spend what's left of the night there.'

'Evan . . .' she whispered into the shoulder of his jacket, 'I'm all right now.'

'So I see,' he said ironically, holding her away from him at last and scanning her white face and trembling lips.

'But . . .'

'No buts,' he said firmly as he laid her gently back against her seat. 'It's not far.'

Half an hour later they were in a warm, cheerful and comfortable motel room with twin beds, and miraculously considering how late it was, Evan had procured hot coffee and some brandy.

'This makes it twice in one day that I've scared you stiff,' he said as he handed her a neat brandy and guided the glass to her lips with a hand on her wrist. 'A record even for me.'

'It wasn't your fault,' she murmured, and grimaced as the brandy went down. But at the feeling of warmth it generated within, she took another sip and then another and some colour began to steal back into her cheeks.

He studied her for a moment, then poured himself one and sat down. 'Do you—ever have nightmares about the accident?'

'Sometimes,' she admitted.

'Ever told anyone?'

'No. But I don't get them nearly as often nowadays.'

'But you still don't like to drive at night.'

She was silent, staring down at her glass.

'Meredith?'

She sighed and lifted her lashes.

'Perhaps Gran is right,' he said sombrely. 'You're not ready to be on your own yet.'

'I'm fine normally, Evan,' she said tiredly.

'Are you?' he countered, and leant across abruptly to pick up her wrist again. 'You're too thin, for one thing.'

She looked down at his long, tanned fingers circling her wrist and shivered suddenly. For it did look thin and fragile within his grip. But not only that, the feel of his hand on it sent a strange tingling up her arm.

'I wasn't ever fat,' she said, pulling free.

'I know.'

She licked her lips and picked up her glass. 'Are we going to share this room?'

Evan sat back. 'It seemed like a good idea at the time. I thought it would be better for you not to be alone. But I can . . .'

'No,' she broke in. 'It's all right. It's only for a few hours anyway.'

He smiled with sudden amusement. 'I guess that says it all. Drink up,' he added, and surprised her by helping her to her feet. 'Do you want to change?'

Meredith looked down confusedly at the fleece-lined grey tracksuit she had put on for the journey. 'I don't think so. I'll just lie down under the cover.'

'Sure you're all right?'

'Yes,' she whispered, but silent tears welled suddenly and

coursed down her cheeks. 'No, I am,' she protested weakly. 'I ... it ... I haven't cried for such a long time I must be making up for it.'

'It doesn't matter.'

But as he held her close in the protective circle of his arms and she wept into his shoulder, she couldn't help thinking dimly how strange it was that Evan of all people should be comforting her and making her gradually feel safe.

And finally she lifted her head and said huskily, 'Thanks.'

His grey eyes held hers for a long time and her lips parted. Then he released her abruptly, but only to pick her up and put her on the bed and sit down beside her to take her shoes off. 'To tell the truth,' he said casually as he pulled the cover up, 'I'm as tired as hell too. Goodnight, Meredith.'

'Goodnight.'

Two minutes later the light went out and she heard the other bed creak. Then there was silence.

The room was flooded with daylight when she woke, and she blinked at the brightness, and realised Evan was sitting on the other bed, shaved and showered and watching her.

She sat up hastily and winced and rushed into speech to cover it. 'Is it very late? You should have woken me earlier.'

'No, it's not that late,' he interrupted. 'But I've just ordered breakfast and it will be here in about ten minutes.'

'Do we have time? I mean ...'

'I've also been on the phone to Chris. He's at the hospital with Gran. Her condition is about the same, but I've told him to tell her that you'll be there soon. Would you like to shower and change in the mean time? I brought your case in.'

'Yes. Yes, I will.' But she didn't move, for the simple

reason that she knew her leg was going to play up as it sometimes did on cold mornings or after having been cramped in one position for any length of time, and she was curiously loath for Evan to be witness to it. This struck her as a little odd, because after the car accident which had claimed Leigh's life and caused her injuries that had left some doubt whether she would ever walk again, he had seen her far less mobile.

But although he got up it was only to walk over to the window, and she gritted her teeth and swung her legs to the floor. Once up on her feet, though, she only got half way to the bathroom and had to stop and lean against the wall.

'What is it?'

Meredith lifted her head at his sharp query. 'Nothing.'

'Don't be an idiot! It's your leg, isn't it? I thought you were over the worst,' he said.

She pushed a hand through her hair and would have given anything to be able to stand upright. 'I am.'

He swore beneath his breath and came over to her. 'It doesn't look like it to me. Why haven't you done something about it, *told* someone at least?'

'Evan,' she interrupted with an effort, 'honestly, there's nothing to tell. All it needs is time now and this doesn't happen often. I'll be fine after I've had a shower.'

'How the hell you expect to shower if you can't stand upright is a mystery to me, Meredith.'

She stared up at him, then turned her cheek to the wall briefly because there was so much anger in those blazing grey eyes, it made her feel helpless, and something else she couldn't put a name to. Why still *so* angry? she wondered bleakly.

Then she took a breath and pushed herself away from the wall. 'I can manage. It only needs loosening up. I've got some exercises. But would you . . . could you get my case, please?'

A nerve flickered in his jaw and she thought for a moment he was going to say something violent, but he looked away suddenly, and when he looked back all that pent-up savagery was wiped from his expression. 'Here,' he said taking her arm, 'lean on me. Does walking loosen it up?'

'Well, yes.'

'Then we'll walk. Hang on.' And he walked her backwards and forwards across the room several times, until she said a little shakily, 'There, it's coming right now.'

'Let me see.'

She let go of him and managed to walk across the room. 'Does it hurt?' he asked, examining her face critically. 'Not much.'

'You're not a very good liar, Meredith. Or rather, it must be the opposite, because I had no idea you were still in such pain. You've hidden it very well.'

'I'm not, really I'm not now, Evan. It's only times like this,' she said anxiously. 'And it will go away in a minute. I couldn't do all the things I can do now, ride, even run if I have to now, otherwise,' she said wryly.

He stared at her. Then he said softly. 'Oh hell,' and walked across the room to take her in his arms, 'there are some things I can't help admiring about you, Merry.'

They stood like that for a moment or two. Then Evan pushed her away to arm's length abruptly and said in a different voice, 'Take your time. We don't want another accident.' And she knew that nothing had changed at all.

A few minutes later, she was standing in the shower with the warm water streaming over her body and the last vestiges of stiffness in her leg waning. She had been incredibly lucky, they had told her after the accident—to have survived at all had been a miracle, to have escaped any significant scarring another. And finally to have won the long hard fight back to full mobility, that had not been a miracle, although she was often tempted to think it one. But it had really been a combined effort—medical skill and care and then a lot of care and encouragement from Mrs Sommerville. But perhaps it had been a miracle after all, to have come so close to being a paraplegic.

She shivered in spite of the warm water and forced herself to remember some of her triumphs. Like finally being able to ride again, which she still did cautiously and only on Nuriootpa, who was almost human in her understanding of a rider and had grown to know Meredith's mind almost before she did. So many little things too, that you never appreciate being able to do until you can't.

And the fact that one leg was still weaker and prone to play up from time to time didn't really bother her. It had been the one trapped in the wreckage, which hadn't helped.

And perhaps because she was thinking of her triumphs, Meredith found herself thinking of Evan again. Because during those long months of recovery, she had seen in his eyes what he had expressed just now—admiration. But it had been unwilling admiration, and although there had been no war of words in those invalid and semi-invalid days, that unwitting look of admiration had nearly always been replaced by something colder.

She shivered again suddenly and wrapped her arms around her slender, wet body, then stepped out of the shower and found herself staring at her cloudy reflection in the long mirror behind the door—only to close her eyes almost immediately, and turn away.

'My darling Merry,' Chris Sommerville said, 'what a delight to see you! But where *were* you?'

'It doesn't matter, Chris,' Evan said tersely to his younger brother. 'And for God's sake stop clutching her like that,' he added irritably. 'How is Gran?'

Chris Sommerville was very tall and very thin and, unlike Leigh or Evan, had dark hair and dark eyes which he was fond of blaming on the fact that he must have been the son of a travelling salesman. Nothing is sacred to that boy, Mrs Sommerville had often said worriedly in Meredith's hearing, and the more she had got to know Chris, the more she had had to agree with this. She had also heard Evan accusing him of being a useless, irresponsible layabout who didn't know how to do a day's work and was hopelessly addicted to slow horses, fast cars and fast women. Even Leigh, she had heard Evan say, had done *something* with his life.

But Chris had only agreed sweetly that he was all of those things and probably some more that his brother didn't know about—although, he had added, if you looked at his punting averages over a period of *time* they weren't quite so . . . well, dismal, and anyway, since when had Evan become a Puritan?

Meredith had not been privy to what Evan had replied. But for all that, she couldn't help liking Chris, and had to laugh at his irreverent sense of humour, his unabashed taste for very voluptuous ladies some of whom had been brought to Sommerville with the express intention of shocking everyone to the core, she had suspected. She had certainly detected the laughter in his eyes more than once.

She also suspected that behind his languid façade there

lurked a shrewd brain and, more, that Chris was unusually perceptive.

He said now, 'Since Gran has learnt that Meredith is to be returned to her side, she does seem to be more peaceful.'

All the same, Meredith was shocked to see how frail and shrunken and grey Mrs Sommerville looked.

'Mrs Sommerville,' she whispered. 'It's me, Meredith.'

'Meredith.' It was a bare thread of sound and those grey eyes that were so like Evan's looked up at her hazily. Then they sharpened and filled with tears. 'Oh, Meredith, I was so worried about you, my dear. Are you all right? Your leg . . .?'

'I'm fine,' Meredith assured her. 'I . . .' She bit her lip and glanced guiltily at Evan, hating herself for what she had done.

'Meredith decided she needed a real holiday, Gran,' he said. 'She went up north.'

'To the seaside?' Mrs Sommerville said, apparently accepting this, although what she said next made Meredith flinch within. 'And I've spoilt your holiday and done the very thing I was so sure I wouldn't! I'm sorry!'

'No. No, *I* am. I should have let you know. But I'm back now and we're going to get you well again.'

Mrs Sommerville stared at her, then at Evan, who said, 'I'm very relieved to have Meredith back too, Gran.'

Mrs Sommerville closed her eyes and seemed to sigh as if the weight of the world had been lifted from her shoulders. And her thin hand crept into Meredith's. 'I seem to be feeling much better already,' she murmured.

All the same, it was nearly a week before the doctor pronounced her out of danger, and nearly a month before she was allowed to go home to Sommerville, and only then with a full-time nurse and the prospect of some weeks still partially bedridden.

Meredith took up residence at the Sommervilles' Newcastle house which Chris was principally inhabiting since taking over the running of the Sommerville Corporation from Evan. It was a large old mansion, handy for the hospital, and she and Chris and Evan could live in it without ever running into each other virtually, if they so wished.

And although she spent most of her time at Mrs Sommerville's bedside, in that month she came to know more of Newcastle, and to appreciate it better. Being New South Wales's second oldest city, it had plenty of history to offer and when one got to know it, she discovered, one could see beyond its commercial and industrial cloak that had always tended to put her off slightly. Not that you could doubt its industrial affiliations—its giant port handled the shipping of coal from the Hunter Valley minefields—but it also had good surfing beaches, a number of theatres and art galleries, some lovely parks and some fine restaurants.

It was to one such restaurant that Evan took Meredith and Chris on the evening of the day they had learnt that Mrs Sommerville was out of danger.

Meredith put on the one good dress she had brought away from Sommerville with her, a cream crêpe garment with a dropped waist, long fitted sleeves, padded shoulders and a cowl neckline. It was the essence of elegance and simplicity, and Mrs Sommerville had bought it for her about twelve months before. Despite her age, Evan's grandmother had a great interest in clothes and fashion and had declared that as soon as she had laid eyes on the dress she had been able to visualise Meredith, and only Meredith, in it.

With it, Meredith wore very pale, patterned stockings and low-heeled cream kid shoes. A slim, rectangular leather purse completed the outfit and all the jewellery she wore was a pair of emerald earrings—a gift from Leigh.

She had washed her hair and brushed it back from her forehead, tucking it behind her ears into a dark gold curve on her shoulders.

But as she stared at her reflection, she wondered if the hairstyle wasn't somehow too revealing. It showed off her oval face to perfection, and the earrings, she thought a shade wryly, yet it did seem to make her look younger and —more vulnerable? she pondered. Or is it that I sometimes tend to hide behind my hair—use it to shadow my face, sort of? In which case I should leave it as it is. Anyway, what is there to feel vulnerable about tonight? I'm *so* relieved . . .

'Darling, you look absolutely gorgeous!' Chris said enthusiastically as she came downstairs. 'Doesn't she, Evan?'

Evan looked up briefly from the drink he was pouring and raised his eyebrows slightly. 'Yes. Would you like a sherry, Meredith?'

'Thank you.'

'Yes,' Chris mimicked, carrying the crystal glass across to Meredith. 'Yes, it was a nice day. Yes, it would be a pity if Japan could get their coal cheaper from South Africa, yes . . .'

'Chris,' Meredith said in an undertone.

But Chris was not to be deterred. 'I am merely apologising for my brother's singularly expressionless way of greeting a marvel of nature and style.'

'Chris,' Evan interrupted, 'Meredith looks lovely. Satisfied?'

'Well, I suppose coming from you that is praise indeed,

Evan. I do know what high standards you have. Are *you* satisfied with that, Merry?' His dark eyes danced impishly.

'Oh God,' Evan remarked wearily but with a faint grin, 'if you're going to be like this all night, we might leave you at home. Meredith,' he transferred his grey gaze to her and a little flame of pure mockery lit his eyes briefly, 'you do look gorgeous, and I mean that. Satisfied.'

'Oh *yes*,' she said huskily. 'I only wish I could press that compliment in my diary so that even when the words have faded, I'll be able to remember this moment.'

Yet, although she had intended to answer the mockery in Evan's eyes, the news they had had earlier in the day must have had the power to sweep away the undercurrents, because suddenly they were all three laughing and Evan even raised his glass to her and murmured, '*Touché*.'

In fact, she found herself viewing *both* her brothers-in-law with something like affection in those moments. Which is *something* of a miracle, she reflected, as she sipped her sherry and they talked idly. But she couldn't help noticing that there was also something more relaxed in the set of Evan's broad shoulders than she had seen since Ballina.

Then it was time to leave, and they took two cars in case Chris wanted to stay out later, but he insisted on having Meredith with him, saying, 'They don't *know* she's my sister-in-law, do they?'

'Who?' Evan enquired.

'Whoever happens to see us, of course.'

'Of course! How silly of me,' murmured Evan. 'Just drive carefully.'

'I don't think Evan will ever look upon me as a man,' Chris said mournfully, as he drove with extra care. 'Do you think so, Merry?'

Meredith hesitated. 'Perhaps older brothers are like that, Chris.'

'Well, I know some who couldn't give a damn! It's a funny thing, but he didn't give much of a damn about Leigh. Know what he said—it doesn't upset you to talk about Leigh, does it, Merry? No. Good. Well, when he finally found out you two were married, he said—it was bound to happen, with that *very* expressive way he sometimes has of shrugging his shoulders to let you know he doesn't give a damn. Now if *I* rushed off and married a complete stranger, however beautiful, I'm sure there'd be hell to pay!'

A secret little smile curved Meredith's lips as she thought of some of Chris's lady loves. But she said gravely, 'Maybe it's just the penalty of being the baby of the family, Chris.'

'Some baby,' he retorted rather acidly. 'I'm twenty-six!'

'I know,' Meredith replied soothingly.

'And you're the baby of the family now, anyway. A mere twenty-two,' he mocked.

'Going on twenty-three.'

'And quite capable of making me feel like a grubby schoolboy too, Merry!'

'Oh now, Chris, I do not!' she protested.

'Well, you laugh at me secretly sometimes—now come on, admit it!'

'I also like you very much!'

He looked considerably mollified and then leant over and kissed her on the cheek. 'Same here, Merry. What started this?' he asked comically.

'You were saying you didn't think Evan would ever treat you like a man. I must say, though, *I* didn't think *you* cared much for what Evan thought or anyone else.'

'That's right, I don't,' Chris said after a moment, with a

happy grin. 'Thanks for reminding me. Here we are!'

Evan was waiting for them outside the restaurant, and he eyed them suspiciously as they walked up because they were still laughing.

'I don't really trust you in this mood,' he said lightly to Chris, however.

'Oh, it's nothing, dear brother,' said Chris, but with such a mysterious air, Meredith had to laugh again.

And that lovely feeling of fun stayed with her for some time.

The restaurant was dim and luxurious with burgundy-coloured velvet-covered chairs, pink damask tablecloths, white carnations on each table and candles. There was a small dance-floor but as yet no band, just some quiet piped music in the background.

Meredith chose a seafood meal, oysters followed by Lobster Mornay, and it was superb. And thanks to Chris, the conversation was lively—or perhaps I'm feeling quite light-headed myself, she mused.

Then Chris spotted some acquaintances across the room and went over to talk to them.

Meredith declined dessert and in the silence, glanced at Evan through her lashes.

'What is it?' he asked quietly, intercepting that glance in the candlelight.

'I—I was just thinking how long it is since I've done anything like this.' Which was true, although not what she had been thinking.

Evan twisted the stem of his wine-glass between his long fingers and said after a time, 'You should do it more often. I don't think I've ever seen you so relaxed.'

'Ah, but there's a special reason for it tonight, isn't there?' she murmured, and sipped her wine.

He studied her across the candle flame with the glow reflected in his grey eyes, making them impossible to read.

'True,' he agreed. 'And I have to thank you for what you've done for my grandmother over the past few weeks. I've no doubt it helped her to turn the corner.'

'Don't . . .'

'Don't what?'

'Thank me. It was the *least* I could do.'

The waiter came and refilled their glasses, and the band struck up with some soft mood music. Meredith watched some couples drift on to the floor and then Evan said, taking her completely by surprise, 'Would you like to dance?'

'I . . . I don't think so,' she stammered.

He looked at her interrogatively, and she stared helplessly at his strong, tanned face and thick fair hair above the snowy white of his shirt, then her glance slid away to his hands lying on the pink tablecloth, and she trembled inwardly.

'Meredith?'

'It's something I haven't tried since . . .' She stopped abruptly.

'Is there any reason why you shouldn't try it?' he queried. 'Do you have a list of forbidden activities in other words?'

'No. Not any more, but . . .'

'All the more reason to, then. Come.' He stood up and held out his hand to her.

'You don't have to do this, Evan.' Her hazel eyes were wide and wary.

His lips twisted. 'And you don't have to look like that, Merry. We made a bargain, didn't we? You could look upon it as my contribution to your rehabilitation, if you liked.'

She lowered her lashes defensively, and said reluctantly, 'All right.' But she shrank inwardly from the feel of his hand on hers and immediately regretted giving in. I should have just said no, she thought. What a fool I am! But I didn't want to spoil the mood of this evening, I think.

Evan asked a few minutes later, 'Is your leg hurting?'

'No.'

'Then let go,' he commanded softly. 'Try not to be so tense.'

How can I? something within cried, but she bit her lip and forced herself to relax. Not much later, she was wondering how she had achieved it. Was it because Evan was a good dancer and he held her firmly but without attempting to smother her? Was it the music which she loved? Or perhaps it was even glimpsing Chris, doing a double-take as they danced by which made her want to laugh. We never fooled him, did we, she thought with that secret smile curving her lips.

'Are you going to let me in on the joke?' Evan asked wryly.

'Oh!' She glanced upwards swiftly and coloured faintly. 'Not a joke but ... well, it was nothing, really.'

A glimmer of amusement lit his grey eyes. 'I saw it too,' he said. 'My unshockable younger brother was distinctly stunned. I think we really might have achieved something tonight, Meredith. There,' he stopped dancing as the last notes of the music faded away, 'was that so bad?' He held her loosely and stared down at her.

'No,' she whispered, and couldn't tear her eyes away from his.

But Chris materialised beside them as the band struck up

again. 'My turn now,' he said. 'You go and dance with Sarah Healey, Evan. Did you know she arrived a few minutes ago with a party? Well, she did. Merry, may I?'

'You may not, Chris,' Evan said deliberately, to both Meredith's and Chris's surprise.

'But . . .'

'This is the first time Meredith's danced since the accident, Chris, so we're not going to overdo it. And if you would kindly get out of my way, I'll take her back to the table. Ask Sarah if she'd like to come over.'

Chris looked mutinous for a moment, then he looked at Meredith, and perhaps her feeling of confusion was mirrored in her eyes, because he then saluted Evan.

'Ay, ay, sir!'

Which caused Evan to say irritably, 'You do realise you're making a spectacle of us?'

'I'm going, I'm going,' said Chris hastily, and left them.

'I'm fine really,' Meredith said uncertainly.

Evan looked down at her. 'Did you want to dance with him particularly?' he asked a little mockingly.

'No—I didn't mean that. And you're right, I probably shouldn't overdo it. I . . .' She floundered, not sure what she meant, and swallowed. 'I mean—thanks, I guess. Once again,' she said huskily then. 'It's becoming a habit,' she added, and flinched visibly as she thought, oh God! Why did I say *that*?

But if he guessed she was remembering a certain conversation they had had about her habits, he gave no sign of it. In fact he said formally, 'It was a pleasure.'

Then they were back at the table and as he pulled out her chair, a stunning brunette tapped him on the shoulder and said, 'Darling! Chris has told me the fabulous news. I'm so happy for you all!'

Evan turned to her and there was a look of affection and something else in his eyes as he took her in his arms and kissed her. 'Thank you, Sarah,' he said, releasing her without haste. 'I rang you to let you know, but you weren't at home.'

Sarah Healey, who Meredith judged was in her late twenties, wrinkled her charming little nose and said with a grimace, 'Daddy whisked me off to a wine-tasting in Sydney. I told him I'd rather be on hand in case anything . . . well, that's behind us now, but he just wouldn't take no for an answer!'

'The penalty for having gained such a reputation in that area,' Evan said humorously.

'I suppose so. Then I rang your place this evening, *and* the hospital to tell you I'd accepted this invitation ages ago and couldn't get out of it, but it seemed as if there was a positive dearth of Sommervilles! I understand why now.'

'Yes. Sarah, I don't think you've met my sister-in-law Meredith?'

For a moment Sarah Healey's great dark eyes looked totally disconcerted. 'Your . . .?'

'Leigh's wife—widow,' Evan murmured, and for some reason looked down at Meredith.

Sarah put a hand to her mouth fleetingly. 'Of course!' she said embarrassedly. 'I'm so sorry, but I wasn't here when Leigh died or . . . and Evan doesn't ever mention you . . . oh dear,' her eyes twinkled suddenly, 'I'm making a complete mess of this, aren't I? Do forgive me, Meredith. I'm very happy to meet you!'

Meredith could never remember what she said in reply, but it must have been acceptable because Sarah sat down with them for several minutes and they chatted amiably. But all the while she was thinking, was that designed to put

me in my place because I was never one of them? And
because it's unthinkable, although Chris may joke about it,
to marry outside the charmed circle of wealth and position
as Leigh did when he married me? Or was it a genuine
lapse because Evan does make a practice of *never* talking
about Leigh's widow? Unfortunately, whatever it is, it
makes me feel like a shadow on the wall. But then I should
be used to that. Only I feel worse. Why, I wonder?

She discovered why on the way home not much later.
Chris, as he had predicted, decided to stay on, but Evan
declined Sarah's host's invitation for them to join the party
too—to Meredith's secret relief.

She said in the car, 'If you would have liked to stay, I
wouldn't have minded.'

'No,' he said decisively, and when she looked at him
curiously, he added, 'I'm going up to Sommerville first
thing in the morning. Anyway, I feel as if I need a good
night's sleep.'

'I know what you mean,' she murmured. 'She's . . . very
attractive, Sarah Healey.'

'Mmm. Very bright too.'

'Oh?'

'Yes. She's not only got a growing reputation as wine-
taster but she's been studying overseas marketing methods
and come home with some brilliant ideas.'

'Your grandmother wondered if you were thinking of
marrying her,' said Meredith, and for the life of her,
couldn't imagine why.

Evan Sommerville's lips twisted into a wry smile. 'Did
she?'

'I shouldn't have revealed that,' Meredith said hastily. 'It
just slipped out.'

'I won't tell her. But in fact the thought has crossed my

mind,' he said idly, and nosed the car into the garage.

A good night's sleep, Meredith thought, staring into the darkness. Oh God, what would I give for a good night's sleep tonight? What did he say earlier . . . I think we might have really achieved something, tonight, Meredith. How right you were, Evan, but if only you knew!

CHAPTER THREE

'I FEEL like a different person already!' Mrs Sommerville smiled, looking round her bedroom. 'How wonderful it is to be home! Don't you feel the same, Meredith?'

'Yes,' said Meredith, and thought, that's true in a way. I hadn't realised how much I would miss Sommerville until I came back. 'Are you comfortable, Mrs Sommerville?'

'Perfectly, thank you, dear. My very efficient nurse has seen to that. She may not make the most scintillating conversation,' she added with a mischievous look at the very plump, middle-aged lady who had been appointed her full-time nurse, 'but she's very good at making me comfortable. More to the point, is she comfortable, do you think?' she asked anxiously. 'I mean, she will be stuck out here for some time.'

'I've had Mrs Whittington move a television set into her bedroom, and she said she loved the view of the rose garden. She also asked me to call her Violet instead of Nurse Jenkins, told me if I needed any physio on my leg, she'd be happy to help, although how she knew about it *I* don't know, and she wondered if she might come down and see the horses sometimes.'

Mrs Sommerville laughed. 'No problems there, then. But I'm sure you deputise most capably for me, Meredith. Will you mind having to do that for quite some time?'

'Not at all,' Meredith said. 'Now . . .'

'No!' Mrs Sommerville said firmly.

'But you don't know what I was going to say.'

'I do know, however, that you've spent too much time lately chained to my bedside. In fact you've probably undone all the good your holiday did you, because you're looking rather pale again. So off you go and don't let me see you for the rest of the afternoon! You must be dying to say hello to Nuriootpa anyway. Not to mention Nhulunbuy and Nunawadding—can *you* tell me why Leigh had such a passion for calling his horses with names starting with N?'

'No,' Meredith said with a grin.

'I'm surprised he didn't want to rename you!'

Meredith turned away and the smile faded, to be replaced by a sudden look of pain. But when she turned back, her face was normal again. And she walked over to the bed and dropped a light kiss on Mrs Sommerville's brow, saying cheerfully, 'You may be able to get rid of me for the afternoon, but I'll be back!'

It was a clear, cool afternoon with the feel to it as if winter was lurking just around the corner.

Meredith breathed deeply and urged Nuriootpa into a canter. The grey mare needed no second invitation and Meredith said to her, 'I suppose no one's had time to exercise you much, have they, old girl? But your mama's home now and against all expectations, here to stay for some time so you can forget that rather tearful farewell we had some weeks ago. But I've got the feeling I'm going to need your company more than ever.'

Nuriootpa twitched her ears almost as if she were human, and Meredith had to laugh. But it was a husky laugh and inexplicably, dangerously close to tears, and she tightened her slender fingers around the reins. Careful, she warned herself. We've had it all out, haven't we? There's nothing to be done but grin and bear it. Anyway, who's to say what it is, really?

She came home from her ride with her cheeks pink and her hair flying, and by a stroke of misfortune, chose to take the narrow walk around the old winery. Which was how, as she came round the corner of the building, she nearly ran down Evan. He had evidently just come out of the building and Meredith found herself having to pull Nuriootpa up so precipitately that the mare reared high in the air.

'Sorry,' she said breathlessly, only having just managed to retain her seat, and having the dubious pleasure of seeing Evan shoot out a hard hand to grab the mare's bridle as if she'd lost control. 'I've never seen anyone in the winery,' she added, 'which is why I took the corner rather fast, I guess.'

He studied her in silence for a minute, then released Nuriootpa and said, 'Then you'll have to get out of that habit. Happy to be home?'

'I ... yes, actually,' she replied in some confusion. 'What ...'

But he cut her off. 'I've been meaning to ask you something. Would you mind if I rode Nhulunbuy? I've decided to put my old hack out to pasture and ...'

'No, of course not,' she interrupted. 'You didn't have to ask.'

'Well, Leigh did leave them to you,' he said with a slight smile.

'Yes, but I have no need of three. As a matter of fact, I'd be rather glad if you did take over Nhulunbuy. I don't ride him myself. Leigh used to say it would be years before he'd have him properly trained as a jumper, if ever. He's got an excess of spirit.'

'I gathered that. Do you jump Nuriootpa?'

'No. Which is a shame really,' she said, patting the mare's neck. 'She jumps like a bird and loves it. Perhaps . . .'

'I wouldn't,' he said. 'It could be dangerous for you. But now that I'm home I'll take her over a few if you like.'

Meredith slid off Nuriootpa's back. 'Thank you,' she said quietly.

Evan glanced at her, his grey eyes curious. 'Have I offended you?'

'No. How?'

'You tell me.'

'You haven't.'

'By saying that it would too dangerous for *you* to jump her, Merry,' he said with a tinge of impatience.

'Why should that offend me? It's probably true.'

'Then you don't like me to be concerned for you?'

No, I don't, she thought with a flash of insight and amazement that he should have been so quick to detect it— before she had, almost.

'Why not?' he queried when she didn't answer.

She shrugged. 'I don't really know. Just . . . stupidity, probably. I think I ought to be getting back.'

'I'll walk down to the stables with you,' he said.

They walked in silence through the gathering dusk until Meredith asked, 'What did you mean when you said I'd have to get out of that habit?'

'Nothing else to be on the defensive about,' he countered.

'I'm not, just puzzled,' she said evenly. 'I am a perfectly safe rider, normally, and it's true that no one ever goes in there—normally.'

'That's what I meant—that will be changing shortly.'

Meredith stopped walking and turned to stare up at him bewilderedly. 'You mean . . .?'

'Yes, I'm planning to start making wine again—rather,

I've never done it before, but I intend to make it my new project. Why do you think I came home to Sommerville?'

The reins slid through Meredith's suddenly nerveless fingers, but Nuriootpa only moved away to the verge and dropped her head to crop the grass.

'You don't have to look so shattered, Meredith,' said Evan, his grey eyes amused and wry. 'Did you imagine I'd come back expressly to make your life a misery?'

She licked her lips. 'I had no idea why you'd come back, but I didn't expect this or that you were interested, to be honest. I mean, you've never spoken of it or . . .' She trailed off, still looking incredulous.

He smiled quizzically. 'Perhaps you just don't know me very well.'

'I don't, obviously,' she said drily, and turned to pick up the reins.

'As a matter of fact you're right,' he said on a different note, a moment later. 'It's not really a burning desire of mine, although I'm sure I'll find it interesting.'

'Then why?' she asked, and turned back to look at him uncertainly.

He raised an eyebrow and shrugged. 'Like Everest, it's there, for one thing. Then there's the challenge of producing a good Upper Hunter wine—and if you really want to know, I've found myself in the throes of a sort of spiritual drought recently. Nothing I've been doing seems like any kind of a challenge any more. Which indicated, I thought, the need for a few drastic changes in my life.'

'Well, I know what you mean,' said Meredith, although dazedly.

He shot her a keen, pure grey glance. 'Do you?'

'I know about spiritual droughts, anyway,' she answered

barely audibly. 'But,' she hesitated, then went on in a normal voice, 'it will take years, won't it?'

'Possibly, although we can start with the existing vines and grapes we've previously sold. But I'm planning new plantings of different types of grapes and it takes four to five years to get a viable crop. I'm also,' he added apologetically, 'going into cattle.'

'You're not going to do away with the stud?' she asked wide-eyed.

'No, you can relax about that, Meredith,' he said with a grin. 'But Sommerville has ridden on its back for a long time now. And apart from that, the rest of the property has virtually lain idle. I mean to make every inch of it pay its own way.'

Meredith stared at him. 'I'm sure you will,' she said eventually.

'Do I detect a note of disapproval?' he queried with a suddenly arrogant look.

'I rather like it the way it is,' she murmured. 'It's so beautiful and peaceful. Not,' she added, 'that it's any business of mine.' And she started to walk towards the stables, tugging gently at Nuriootpa.

'Meredith,' he said abruptly, and put a hand on her arm to detain her, 'you can make it your business.'

'How?'

'You could come into partnership with us. I'm forming a new company for the winery. And I intend to make Gran and Chris partners as well as Sarah Healey, although she'll be a working partner—the one with the expertise.'

Meredith blinked. And all she could think of to say was, 'Does Mrs Sommerville *know* about all this?'

Evan smiled faintly. 'Not yet. I really wanted to come home and think it all out first. Then she had the accident.

But I don't suppose she'll object.'

'No, I don't suppose she will.'

'Well?'

Meredith closed her eyes briefly. 'I'd have to think about it, Evan. Quite frankly, I'm a little stunned.' She rubbed her forehead.

'In other words,' he said impatiently, 'you're not *really* willing to accept the bargain I made with you?'

'I've kept my side of the bargain!' she protested.

'Oh yes,' he said harshly. 'But why do I get the feeling you don't want me to keep mine? Is it that you prefer how it was before I tracked you down to Ballina?'

'No,' she breathed, flinching from the hard glitter in his eyes and the uncompromising line of his mouth.

'Then what?' he shot at her. 'Tell me!'

She shivered and tried to back away, but the mare was right behind her. She swallowed and tried to collect her thoughts. 'It's not something I can make up my mind about just like that,' she said helplessly.

'Oh, but I'd like to bet that if you thought about it for a month, your answer would be no, Meredith!'

'That's . . . that's my prerogative, Evan,' she said shakily.

'And yours never to forget too, I gather,' he replied mockingly.

A glitter of anger lit her eyes. 'Up until a very few weeks ago, you made sure I never could forget,' she whispered. 'I'm sorry, but perhaps I just can't accept this change of heart so readily. But may I point out that *you* brought this up, not me.'

'You're wrong, Merry. You bring it up every time you look at me, every time you flinch when you think I'm going to touch you. What do you think I'm going to do, as a matter of interest?' His gaze was sardonic and dispassionate.

'Do? Nothing.' She tried to inject into her voice a semblance of the same detachment. 'Although, as the all-time object of your disgust, until your grandmother nearly died, that is, would it be so unusual for me to be a bit nervous about what you might do?'

'Well, you can relax, my dear,' he said ironically. 'I'd never hurt anyone half as lovely as you.' But although his mood had slipped into another, lighter gear, his eyes probed hers mercilessly, and the mockery in them was plain for all the world to see.

She turned away convulsively, but he turned her back effortlessly. 'Don't do that.'

'Evan . . . oh *hell*!' she said through gritted teeth. 'I told you this couldn't work!'

'But it can, Meredith,' he said quite mildly. 'Provided you stop fighting me every step of the way. And if you take my advice and come in to the winery, I'll make you a lot of money. Think of that!' He trailed his fingers down her cheek to the point of her chin where they stayed for a moment, in a deliberately gentle, featherlight touch. 'Just think of that,' he murmured again, and dropped his hand at last, turned on his heel and walked away.

Meredith stared after him, then when he was out of sight, she buried her face in Nuriootpa's neck and burst into stormy tears.

'Y-you poor thing,' she mumbled at last, and lifted her head. 'I'm always crying into your mane, lately. If you only knew how I wished I could get back to the good old days when I found it impossible to shed a tear!'

Chris came up to spend the next weekend, and Sarah

Healey came to stay too.

Mrs Sommerville had received the news of the wine-making project with enthusiasm and excitement, and had had Nurse Jenkins, now commonly known as Violet, dig out all the family albums and memorabilia, in a bid to track down as much as she could about that earlier Sommerville who had gone to South Africa and come back so enthusiastic about their architecture and wine.

'Oh, it has so much potential to become a real showplace winery!' she said with a glowing look over dinner on Saturday night, which she was attending in her wheelchair. 'Now forgive me, Sarah, I know your father's winery at Pokolbin is one of the oldest and so on, not to mention one of the most famous, but don't you think we have real potential too? I always thought it was *such* a shame that that perfectly lovely building should be standing idle. Can you imagine how it would lend itself to tourist wine-tasting tours which is the in thing, isn't it?'

Sarah Healey laughed. 'You don't have to convince me, Mrs Sommerville. I must say it's very good to be back at Sommerville too.' She glanced expressively at Evan. 'Three years in Europe, although I enjoyed it, has convinced me that there's no place like home!'

'It's very lovely to have you back,' Mrs Sommerville said warmly, and looked up as Violet appeared behind her. 'Oh no, not time for bed, is it, Violet?' she protested.

'It certainly is,' said Violet with a broad beam creasing her plain round face, and Meredith stopped to think that she'd never seen Violet not smiling about something. 'We know what it's like if we get overtired, now don't we?' Violet added coyly. Which caused Chris to roll his eyes and Evan to put his wine glass down irritably.

None of this had the slightest effect on Violet, and she

wheeled Mrs Sommerville out tenderly.

'How can she put up with that woman?' Chris asked.

'God knows,' Evan replied. 'I can't.'

'She takes very good care of your grandmother,' said Meredith thoughtfully.

'Well, that puts us in our place, doesn't it, brother Christian?' drawled Evan.

'Now, Evan!' Sarah chided. 'I'm sure Meredith didn't mean it like that. But I'll go in and spend some time with Mrs Sommerville before she goes to sleep.'

'Do I, do I . . . what do I detect in the air?' Chris said to Meredith about ten minutes later. She had declined coffee and decided to go for a walk. She had only gone a few paces beyond the verandah when Chris had loomed up beside her. And he sniffed the air keenly now.

'What?' she asked with a slight smile.

'W-e-ll, certainly an excess of talk about Chardonnay, Cabernet Sauvignon, Semillon, not to mention Pinot Noir *et* Pinot Blanc,' he said with an exaggerated French accent. 'And laced with black friable loams, salinity, sodicity, calcium carbonates—I tell you, Merry, it's enough to put you off drinking the stuff, much as I like wine!'

'It is all very technical,' Meredith agreed wryly.

'It's bloody boring! I can't imagine what Evan sees in it!'

Meredith was silent. The night air was scented and still and the only sound was the gravel crunching beneath their feet. And the moon was round and yellow—Meredith was always grateful for a yellow moon.

'Then again,' Chris said, 'perhaps I can. Or was I imagining that Sarah has suddenly become . . . possessive?'

'I wouldn't know.'

'Now, Merry,' he replied, 'don't tell me you didn't have

your nose put out of joint back there?'

'I ...'

'Didn't feel that Sarah was usurping your position without so much as a by-your-leave in going to tuck Gran in?'

Meredith bit her lip, then had to laugh softly. She stopped walking and leant back against a railing fence, staring up at the dark sky and jewel-bright stars.

'Chris, you're diabolical,' she said finally.

'But right?'

'Yes, right,' she conceded. 'Which makes me feel a little ridiculous.'

'I wouldn't. It's suddenly dawned on me that Sarah Healey, whom I've known since infancy, might have become one of those subtly *dominating* females. But tell me if I'm not right about something else—has the truce between you and Evan fallen apart?'

'What do you mean?' Meredith asked mechanically.

Chris looked at her reproachfully. 'Darling, I'm not a fool. I've always known there was something,' he lowered his voice dramatically, 'deep and dark between you and Evan. I've even hazarded a guess as to what it might be.'

Meredith tensed. 'You couldn't possibly ...' She stopped abruptly.

'Just let me try this out for size,' he said idly. 'Did Evan ever catch you in compromising circumstances, Merry?'

She gasped and Chris smiled slightly. 'Right again,' he murmured apologetically.

'Chris,' she said with an effort, 'if Evan has ... I don't know how you know this but if Evan ...'

'I didn't, and Evan has not said a word about it to me,' he interrupted. 'It was pure speculation. You see, his dislike of you just didn't seem *rational* to me. Not—*knowing* you and having done so for quite some time now, as he has too. So what, I asked myself, might you have done once to excite such, albeit veiled, animosity in him?'

'I did marry above my station,' Meredith said drily.

'Pshaw!' Chris replied expressively. 'At least, that's my point of view and normally Evan's, I would imagine. We're not royalty. However ...'

'Chris,' Meredith interrupted.

'Just bear with me, Merry,' he said quietly. 'Was it because she married Leigh? I asked myself. What else could it have been unless ... but you and Evan didn't even know each other beforehand, did you? No,' he said to her slight negative movement of her head. 'But why would he object to that so much—I mean, you marrying Leigh? I'm afraid,' he said ruefully then, 'that an answer to that popped straight into my head. Possibly because I've had enough lectures myself from Evan about falling prey to fortune-huntresses.'

Meredith made a sharp, restless movement.

'So, I wasn't wrong. About what Evan *thought*?'

'Please, don't go on,' she whispered.

'Ah, Merry,' Chris said gently, 'I think it's all *gone* on for too long, personally. But just let me finish. Why would he be so convinced of that? All I could come up with was that he'd discovered, somehow, that you hadn't loved Leigh. And that's,' he confessed, 'when my lurid imagination took over. Only I can't really believe that he caught you with another man.'

'I don't know why you don't turn to writing detective stories. Your imagination is very sound,' she said shakily.

'Can't you prove to him that he was wrong, Merry?'

'Oh, Chris,' she answered after a long time, 'thank you for that, but no, I can't.'

'Leigh,' he said musingly, but Meredith put an urgent hand on his arm. 'Don't, Chris. There's no point in taking it any further, and I *really* don't want you to.'

'But how can you go on living like this?'

'I only have myself to blame,' she whispered. Then she straightened up. 'Unfortunately, circumstances have conspired against me—and Evan, I guess. Which is why I'm still here. But it can't last for ever. And in the mean time, we both decided your grandmother was more important than our differences.'

Chris straightened too and they started to walk back to the house. 'All right,' he said finally, having been sunk deep in thought, apparently, 'but just remember this. Gran and I love you very much, each in our own way and whatever. Even if Evan loves to hate you.'

On Sunday, Meredith took things into her own hands. She went in to Mrs Sommerville rather early and spent half an hour with her, then announced that she was driving down to Newcastle for the day.

'Oh?' Mrs Sommerville looked at her a shade sharply.

But Meredith only smiled tranquilly and said, 'I made a friend down there while you were in hospital and I promised I'd pay a visit.'

Mrs Sommerville's brow cleared immediately. 'Well, I'm pleased to hear that, Meredith! Why don't you invite this friend up here some time?'

'I might one day.'

And by a stroke of good fortune, she contrived to miss both Evan and Sarah as well as Chris. Not that she had any reason to be avoiding Chris, yet after the disclosures of the previous night, she wasn't unhappy to be doing so.

Nor had she felt it necessary to tell Mrs Sommerville that

her new friend was only nine years old, the victim of a car accident like herself, and resident in the same hospital that Mrs Sommerville had been in.

She had met Felicity Kenwood on her way to see Mrs Sommerville one day, as the child had been struggling to walk in a walking-frame down the corridor with two nurses aiding and encouraging her, and she had immediately recognised the sheer pain and uncertainty in the child's blue eyes. A pointed, freckled little face and long fair plaits had only added to her vulnerability somehow. Meredith had gone to see the Sister of the ward and discovered that to add to the little girl's trauma, her mother was dead and her father lived on a property way outback, which meant he was only able to see her occasionally. When Meredith had suggested she could visit the child and might even be of some help, having been through something similar herself, the Sister had been delighted.

In the space of a few short weeks Meredith and Felicity had become firm friends.

That she hadn't been forgotten was obvious by the wide, wide smile on Felicity's face when she walked into the ward that Sunday morning, and the warm hug she received.

'Oh, Merry, I'm so happy to see you!'

'Well, I can truthfully say the same, honey. How are you?'

'I'm fine! Sister says I'll be running a marathon soon— but I wish you'd come yesterday!'

'Why?'

'Because Daddy came down to see me and I did want him to meet you!'

'I'm sure he will one day, poppet. Guess what? Sister says I can stay and have lunch with you.'

Meredith came away finally with the usual feeling of tears and warmth in her heart. The children's ward does that to you, a nurse had said to her. They're so darn brave ...

But unfortunately, although she had left herself plenty of time to get back to Sommerville before dark, she had a puncture just past Scone and the only motorist to pass was a quite elderly gentleman who was the soul of courtesy but nearly as feeble as she was when it came to changing tyres. They did it, finally, though Meredith was left facing the last twenty-five miles of the drive in the darkness on a dusty, unlit country road.

She climbed back into the car having waved off her elderly Sir Galahad, who was going in the opposite direction, and took a deep breath. Of course you can do it, she told herself.

And she did it, but after she had garaged her car, she was white with weariness and limping noticeably as she walked up the front steps, to find Evan awaiting her on the verandah, his grey eyes blazing and his mouth taut and hard.

'Where the hell have you been?' he shot at her.

Meredith blinked. 'I went to Newcastle.'

'I know that,' he brushed her words aside curtly. 'I thought you *never* drove in the dark. You do realise you've worried the life out of my grandmother?'

'I'm sorry. I'll go and explain.'

'It's too late for that. Violet,' he said sardonically, 'has already given her a sleeping-pill. So you can explain to me.'

Meredith stared at him steadily. 'I don't have to explain anything to you, Evan,' she said very quietly. 'I don't know why you should imagine I'm accountable to you.'

'All the same, you will,' he said, equally quietly but with a deadly kind of menace.

'You can't make me.'

He laughed, and it was a chilling sound. 'Who is this mysterious friend, to begin with, Meredith?' he drawled.

She stared at him with her lips set.

'Male, perhaps? A boy-friend?' he suggested. 'Someone who's realised what a ripe plum you ...'

Her hand flashed out as a flame of pure anger lit her hazel eyes, but he caught it in mid-air. 'I thought we'd agreed that wasn't a good idea, Merry,' he said quite gently.

'*Don't* call me that,' she gritted through her teeth, and tried, unsuccessfully, to release herself. Then she gasped as her leg gave way momentarily, and he released her wrist to clamp her in his arms.

'I'm all right, let me go!' she breathed, her eyes still furious.

'Sure?' he queried.

'*Yes!*'

'Then,' his eyes mocked her and he made no move to release her, 'if it's going to be open slather again, a romantic interlude that got out of hand seems to me to be the only explanation I can think of to make you subject yourself to driving in the dark.' He raised an enquiring eyebrow at her.

I'll not ... I simply refuse to explain to you, Evan, she thought. Think what you *like*! And she tilted her chin defiantly and disdainfully at him.

Which brought an amused look to his eyes and he said, 'Then if it is going to be open slather again, *Meredith*, why shouldn't I participate? You have the most exquisite mouth, did you know? But I suppose you do.' And he bent his head to kiss her.

Meredith went rigid in his arms. And she twisted her

head away violently. 'Don't you *dare!*' she said in a raging undertone. 'Do you have any idea how much I hate you and despise you, Evan Sommerville? To my mind you're a prime example of the worst type of male chauvinist. If you *think* I'm going to . . . to . . .' she stuttered for a moment, 'to dissolve in your manly arms from desire, you're . . .' She stopped as his hands moved on her body, to caress the small of her back and the curve of her shoulder through the thin stuff of her blouse.

'I think,' he said, on a curiously husky note and with his eyelids half lowered as he watched her mouth, 'that I'm going to kiss you, Merry, and nothing on earth is going to stop me. I'm sorry if you don't approve, but that's the way it is.'

'No,' she whispered in the last few moments left to her. 'Evan, no.'

'Yes, Merry.' And his lips closed over hers as his hand slid through her hair to tug it gently.

It was an astonishingly gentle kiss, and she thought afterwards, when she was in a condition to think rationally at last, it was just that gentleness that had floored her and stunned her so completely. And it was only afterwards that she worked out why he should have kissed her like that—a further form of mockery, probably, and anyway, because he was too clever for her . . .

But at the time, all her mind seemed capable of registering was the feel of his arms around her, drawing her slender body into his, bending her back slightly because he was taller—encompassing her spiritually and physically in an embrace and a long searching kiss that, when it finally ended, left her trembling in his arms, devastated at the effect it had had on her.

The only verandah light on cast a pale yellowy glow

over them, and beyond, the sky was a deep velvety blue when his lips left hers and she made a small husky sound of despair in her throat.

'Meredith.' He said her name barely audibly and his breath fanned her forehead.

Her eyes flew open and they stared at each other for a long, frozen moment. Then her lashes dropped, but not before Evan saw the shimmer of tears in her eyes.

He let her go then, but immediately brought his hands up again to steady her. A nerve beat suddenly in his jaw as he said, 'I'm sorry, I shouldn't have done that. But I was worried too. It won't happen again.'

Her lips parted and her eyes were dark and shocked.

'Are you all right?' His hands left her experimentally and he watched her critically.

'I . . . yes,' she breathed.

'Then I'll tell Mrs Whittington you're back. She kept some dinner.'

'Evan,' she said as he turned away.

He stopped and waited.

She licked her lips and swallowed. 'I had a flat tyre. That's why I'm late. It's in the car—you can check. And I went to see a little girl in hospital. I met her when your grandmother was there. She's having to learn to walk again.'

He turned round fully but slowly, and his mouth was set and his expression taut. He said, 'You could have told me. I gave you the chance.' And his grey gaze was merciless.

Meredith looked away. 'You could have trusted me.'

'Oh, I . . .'

But she put out a hand as if to ward off his words—as if to ward off a physical blow—and said his name a little frantically.

'What?' he asked harshly.

'I ... no, it's nothing,' she murmured, and moved restlessly as if to go past him and inside.

'*Say* it, Merry!' he commanded, and blocked her path.

She looked down at her hands and twisted them together, then up at him at last, and her lips quivered as she read the implacability in his eyes. 'All right. I know you don't trust me—can't trust me, but how can you ... how can you?' Her voice sank and she bit her lip and shrugged.

'Want to kiss you in that case?' Evan asked finally.

'Oh, I understand that.' Her eyes were suddenly bitter. 'But not like that. Not the way you did it ... I ...'

Their gazes locked together suddenly. 'Then you liked it?' he murmured. 'Perhaps we *should* try it again if that's the case.'

Meredith bowed her head and her hair fell like a silky gold curtain around her face while he waited and watched. But when she lifted it at last, her eyes were tearless although her face was paler than ever.

'Merry.' His lips barely moved and his eyes had changed.

But she said jerkily. 'I understand, Evan. Can I go in now?'

And Violet chose that moment to appear on the verandah and to say jovially, 'There you are, Mrs Meredith! Everyone was so worried about you, but I told them you'd get home safe and sound!'

Meredith managed to smile at her. 'Thank you, Violet.'

CHAPTER FOUR

'I'M GOING to give a party,' Mrs Sommerville announced to Meredith the next morning, sitting up in bed with her white hair loose and a beautiful mauve cashmere shawl around her shoulders. 'What do you think of that idea?'

'If you ask me, I love parties,' said Violet, removing the breakfast tray from the bed.

'So do I. So do I,' Mrs Sommerville said gravely, but the glance she cast at Meredith was full of laughter. And when Violet had left the room, she added, 'Well, now that we have Violet's approval, what is there to stop us?'

Meredith grinned back. 'Indeed. Are you sure you feel up to it, though?'

'It's worse than that! I feel as if I *need* it, my dear. And anyway I have an excellent excuse with the reopening of the winery to be celebrated. Now, I thought of having it a month from now, which will give us plenty of time to get organised, I thought of a buffet dinner and dancing afterwards so that we can all get out our glad rags, and I—wondered if you would care to be in charge of operations?'

Meredith hesitated, but she noticed that Mrs Sommerville's grey eyes were suddenly anxious. She said, 'I've never done anything like that but,' she paused, but found that she simply could not say what she really felt—that a party at Sommerville was the last thing she felt like organising or attending, 'I guess with your expert advice I might just manage it!'

Mrs Sommerville sighed with relief, then looked a little guilty, which she covered up by saying, 'I knew I could rely

on you, Meredith. Oh, I do believe it will actually do me a
world of good. And I know you will enjoy the kind of party
I have in mind. Now, first the guest-list.'

They spent most of the morning drawing up a guest-list
and wording the invitation for the printers. And certainly
Mrs Sommerville's enthusiasm and the sparkle it brought to
her eyes made Meredith feel that it probably would do her
the world of good, and hoped that none of *her* reservations
would show through.

On top of a virtually sleepless night, though, the effort of
being as enthusiastic herself told, and after lunch, she lay
down on her bed and fell deeply asleep.

It was the sound of an unusual commotion that woke her.
And the sight that greeted her on the side verandah made
her blink and catch her breath in fright.

Evan, whom she hadn't seen all day, was standing
beneath the verandah wall in the rose garden with
Nhulunbuy. The horse was sweating heavily and blowing
and rolling his eyes as he had a habit of doing. Evan was
also sweating and from his expression, furiously angry but
at first impression, also covered in blood.

Meredith made a strangled sound and stumbled down
the stairs. 'What's happened? Are you all right?'

Evan ignored her last question and answered the first,
although obliquely. 'An excess of spirit, you said, didn't
you, Meredith? If ever I've heard an understatement, that's
it. The horse is bloody mad! I'm lucky to be alive.'

At that point both Violet and Mrs Whittington arrived
on the verandah and in a twinkling of an eye Violet took
command—or at least tried to.

'Oh, Mr Sommerville, fallen off your horse, have you?'
she said to him as if he was about ten and accident-prone.
'Never mind, I'll fix you up.'

But this was the last straw as far as Evan was concerned,

apparently. 'You stay away from me, Violet!' he commanded through his teeth, and sent her a grey glance that would have stopped a tank in its tracks.

'But you're bleeding, Mr Evan,' Mrs Whittington protested.

'It's nothing,' Evan said curtly, and Meredith, from her closer vantage, realised that it was mainly a long graze down his arm and a cut on his temple and that he wasn't in any danger of bleeding to death. 'I'll take him,' she said, and put a hand on the reins. Whereupon Nhulunbuy neighed shrilly and dropped his aristocratic nose into her shoulder as if she were a long-lost relative.

Evan stared at them for a moment, then swore even more furiously and yanked the reins out of her hand. 'What the hell is this? A conspiracy against me?' he demanded.

'Of course not, Evan, but . . .'

'Did he ever throw Leigh, then?'

'Not that I know of, but . . .'

'Has he ever thrown you?'

Meredith took a breath. 'No, but I don't . . .'

'Don't keep saying *but* to me like that, Meredith! Anyway, I'm taking him back to the stables. You do whatever you want to.' And so saying, he wheeled the reluctant horse around and strode off with him, wreaking further havoc amongst the beds of early primulas that surrounded the roses.

Meredith counted to ten beneath her breath and looked up at the verandah. Violet winked at her and motioned with her hand that Meredith should follow Evan. Even Mrs Whittington who ran the household superbly but rather like an expressionless shadow in the background was grinning.

Meredith grinned back feebly and thought, it's all very well for you two to laugh—well, it *is* rather funny really, and I suppose I'd better go and try to find out exactly what did happen.

She had her amusement well under control by the time she caught up with Evan, and she walked beside him in silence for a way. Then she said, 'He was very fresh.'

Evan didn't reply.

'I'll put him away,' Meredith suggested as they reached the stable complex, and he handed the reins to her silently but with ceremonious satire.

She led the horse off to a washbay and hosed him down, then dried him and handed him over to a stablehand to walk him for a while. By the time she got back to the stable office into which Evan had disappeared he was sitting behind a battered desk with a bottle of Dettol in front of him and some cotton wool. Neither had been used. However, the bottle of Scotch also on the desk had its lid off and Evan was lying back in the chair with his feet up on the desk, drinking from a battered tin mug.

He eyed her for a moment, then said, 'Care to join me?'

'No, thank you.' She looked around and located the rest of the first-aid stuff that was kept in the office for just such emergencies, and took a shallow bowl over to the sink to fill it with water.

It was as she was adding Dettol to the water that Evan said, 'Don't tell me *you're* going to minister to me, my dear Meredith?'

'Not if you don't want me to,' she replied evenly.

'I didn't say that.'

'You didn't have to,' she murmured, and found herself wanting to laugh again and marvelling that she should, considering all that had passed between herself and Evan. 'But perhaps I should point out,' she said gravely, 'that you have three choices. You can do it or I can do it or Violet can do it. Of the three of us I can guarantee that Violet would do the best job . . .'

'And relish every minute of it,' he broke in ironically. 'Heaven preserve me! You'd better do it, then,' he added ungraciously.

Meredith proceeded to do so calmly and impersonally. It took some time to clean up his arm, which he sat through stoically, sipping from the mug from time to time. But when she touched her fingertips delicately to the cut on his head, he winced.

'It's not that deep,' she said, 'but it might need a sticking-plaster on it.'

'I'm not going around with sticking-plaster all over me, Meredith,' he said positively. 'Just clean it. I heal well.'

'All right, here goes. There,' she said a few minutes later, 'but you're going to have to have a pad on it whether you like it or not, Evan, just until it stops bleeding anyway. You'll just have to grin and bear it.' She folded a piece of lint and taped it to his forehead.

'You're very determined, aren't you, Meredith?' he observed.

'Not at all. By rights I should probably put a bandage round your head, but I'll spare you that.' She smiled slightly and sat down on the corner of the desk to admire her handiwork.

And that was when she suddenly found it was no longer possible to be impersonal, that she was uncomfortably conscious of his proximity, of the strong line of his broad shoulders beneath his torn, dusty shirt. Of his equally dusty thick fair hair which her fingers had brushed, of the tanned lines of his throat.

She took a quick uncertain breath and went to turn away, but he put out a hand and caught her wrist, and her eyes flew to his apprehensively and guiltily before she could stop herself.

'Meredith,' he said very quietly, his fingers moving on the soft inner skin of her wrist, 'you know what's going to happen to us one day, don't you?'

She stared at him, her lips parted and with a pulse beating erratically at the base of her throat. And with that forbidden image flooding her mind—herself in his arms, lying against the long, strong length of him, naked and luxuriously abandoned ...

'There are some things that can't be denied,' he went on in that same deep, quiet voice. 'You must know what I'm talking about,' he added, his eyes challenging hers.

'No,' she breathed.

'You don't?'

She lowered her lashes. 'Yes. But no, it's not going to happen, Evan,' she whispered.

'You *say* that, but some of the things you do lead me to think otherwise.'

She winced inwardly. 'Some of the things *you* do leave me little choice,' she countered, however.

'Look at me, Merry,' Evan ordered after a moment. And when she did at last, he said, 'It's occurred to me that we're fighting thunder, my dear. Especially after what happened last night.'

It's occurred to me that I'm fighting thunder. The thought slid through her mind and she trembled suddenly so that he felt it through her wrist.

'Meredith?'

'I ...' She licked her lips. 'Evan,' she said huskily, 'I've already made one bad mistake in my life. This would be another. That's why it can't and won't happen.'

'We might find it's not such a mistake.'

She looked downwards and her hair fell forward. 'We ...

for a little while, perhaps,' she conceded. 'But how could it last?' she asked in a low, shaken voice. 'We don't even *like* each other! There are things that have been said and done between us that we could never forgive. There are *people* between us. And I would only despise myself eventually—which you already do. No.'

Evan was silent, still holding her wrist and moving his fingers on it possessively and watching what he was doing rather intently. 'Tell me about one of these people between us, then,' he said, still looking down. 'Tell me about Leigh, Meredith.' And he looked up suddenly, straight into her eyes.

She shivered. 'How *could* I? No.'

'You said just now you had made a bad mistake,' he persisted. 'I presume you meant marrying Leigh. Tell me why, at least.'

She looked at him blindly and saw instead a new-looking headstone in the family graveyard only about half a mile away, on the other side of the winery, one that hadn't weathered or mellowed as much as the others. She saw the silver-framed photos of Leigh in Mrs Sommerville's bedroom and the way her eyes softened and saddened still when she looked at them. And she remembered the day last year on the anniversary of Leigh's death when she'd gone down to the graveyard, to find Evan there ahead of her staring down at the grave with his back to her but grief and pain visible in the taut lines of his body—she had left as quietly as she'd come. She remembered that she had even thought once that they must be a strange family, the Sommervilles, and that they didn't greatly care about each other and how, gradually, she had come to realise that they did, they just didn't show it much.

She came back from those bleak memories and straightened her shoulders. 'It's probably always a terrific gamble to marry for money, Evan,' she said quietly.

He released her wrist and sat back. 'There is such a thing as a statute of limitations even for criminals. One mistake needn't brand you for ever.'

'That's very kind of you, Evan,' she replied ironically, 'but . . .'

'Look, if you won't tell me any different,' he broke in roughly, 'what the hell am I supposed to think?'

'How can I tell you any different?' she asked a little harshly. 'Not you,' she added in a barely audible undertone.

They stared at each other until he said brusquely, 'All right, let's forget it. God knows why I brought it up.' He looked at her scathingly. 'I suppose you've heard about the party?'

She nodded.

'And I presume you'll be staying until then?'

'Yes,' she said uncertainly.

'You don't sound too sure.'

'I . . . it wasn't that,' she said confusedly.

'What was it, then?' he asked, casting her his old, arrogant look.

'Well, I hadn't even thought of leaving before then. I mean, I don't see how I could—not yet.'

Evan smiled, a curiously unpleasant little smile. 'I find that strange,' he drawled. 'Because I've thought of it.'

'Of me leaving?'

'Of one of us leaving. If it's any consolation to you, my dear Meredith, you were probably right.' He flashed her a sardonic grey glance. 'This isn't working very well. But then perhaps you don't mind this—kind of torment so much?'

She flushed and stood up abruptly.

'Meredith?'

'Stop it, Evan,' she whispered.

'Or do you see it as some kind of a victory?'

She took a breath. 'I told you last night what I saw it as—a typically male form of revenge.'

'Ah, but you did qualify that, didn't you? And you did participate in it. Perhaps it's something yet again, Merry,' he said quite gently. 'Are you the kind of woman who enjoys being tormented?'

Meredith gasped and her eyes burned with a flash of anger that swept through her so fiercely, she found she was fighting for breath. 'I . . .' she began, but couldn't speak further. Instead, she snatched up the whisky bottle and lifted it to smash it to the floor, but she changed her mind suddenly and carried it over to the sink and poured it all down the drain, listening with intense satisfaction to the glug-glug it made. Then she walked back to the desk, conscious that Evan was lying back in the chair, watching every move she made, and she slammed the empty bottle down in front of him.

He didn't look at it, just stared up at her quizzically.

Meredith tightened her lips furiously and stormed out of the office.

Is it possible to stay deeply and burningly angry for a whole month? she asked herself on the night of Mrs Sommerville's party.

She was dressing and had just put her robe on over her delicate lace underwear, to do her face and hair.

Her dress was laid out on the bed. She had gone down to Sydney for two days, the week before, to supervise the final stages of Mrs Sommerville's outfit which had been specially made for her, and to find something for herself to wear.

'Well, I was still angry when I bought that,' she

murmured, staring down at the vivid splash of colour on the bed.

The dress was long and fashioned from yellow and gold shot silk. It had no ornamentation—it needed none because the material itself glittered and made such a statement, and the styling was simple. A gathered neckline which could be worn up or pushed below the shoulders, long sleeves gathered into the wrist and a slender gathered skirt. To go with it, she had high, gold kid sandals and she intended to wear it off the shoulder and with no jewellery other than pearl earrings, and with her hair brushed back from her face and loose to her shoulders.

Mrs Sommerville had been wildly enthusiastic but just a little surprised.

'Not quite my usual style,' Meredith had responded wryly.

'My dear, I didn't mean that!' Evan's grandmother had protested. 'You have lovely taste, but normally,' she'd put her head on one side and eyed the shimmering material admiringly, 'understated, if anything.'

'Yes, well, perhaps it's time I made some kind of a statement,' Meredith had murmured, and then pretended she hadn't noticed Mrs Sommerville's look of surprised enquiry. And she wondered to herself what she had actually meant.

She remembered her words now as she stared down at the bed, and thought, did I mean that I was still angry when I bought it? Is it a statement of anger? Perhaps, because I am still angry, with Evan, but even more so with myself.

She turned away from the bed and sat down in front of her dressing-table, staring steadily at her reflection. And wondered if this frighteningly deep, inner pool of rage was visible in her eyes.

But all she could detect was that, if anything, she looked

well, surprisingly well and better possibly than for some time. Her skin was smooth and golden, her hair shone and there seemed to be an indefinable air about her—of decision? she mused, and studied the tilt of her chin. Yes, decision, she decided, and smiled faintly but it didn't reach her eyes. A final and definite resolution then, she added to herself, to put behind me any lingering attraction Evan Sommerville might hold for me. An unalterable acknowledgement that I was mad to let it spring up out of nowhere . . . well, yes, *nowhere*, and mad is to put it mildly. Totally insane is more like it. How could I have let myself succumb like that, however briefly? After everything, to fall into that *trap*. Well, I got my just desserts, she thought bitterly. Not only to have him say what he did but to suggest—and it was tantamount to a suggestion—what he did, when only a few weeks ago he admitted he was thinking of marrying Sarah Healey amongst other things.

She closed her eyes and, a little to her horror, discovered that she still felt like smashing things. That won't do, she warned herself, and winced as she remembered her senseless gesture with the whisky bottle.

Yet, on the other hand, it was her anger that had kept her going, she knew. That had let her go on living in the same house as Evan, in such close contact. It had become a shield and more effective than she had believed possible. It had actually allowed her to sail through the last month, impervious to Evan and to Sarah Healey who was spending more and more time at Sommerville. It had even allowed her to offer Sarah Nunawadding for her personal use and to accept graciously, and genuinely, the amount of time Sarah spent with Mrs Sommerville. And it had certainly helped her to put her heart and soul into organising this party.

'Only,' she murmured to her reflection as she picked up her brush and stroked it through her hair to watch the silky gold strands cling to her brush, 'what next? It's as if this party has become the be-all and end-all of my existence. Where do I go from here, in other words?'

Then she grimaced, not because any solution had presented itself to her but because it struck her as odd that a party she wasn't even very keen to attend should be that.

Mrs Sommerville had compiled the guest-list carefully so that there would not only be close friends of the family present but acquaintances with close interests. Thus it would be a fairly representative gathering of the breeding world from the neighbouring studs, the wine world from both the Upper and Lower Hunter, and the business world from Newcastle. Meredith had recognised many names on the list but had not be able to claim friendship with most— nor had even made their acquaintance. Well, it's high time you did, my dear, Mrs Sommerville had said. Look upon this as your coming out, she had added.

But a few names on the list had rung an elusive bell in Meredith's memory until she had realised she had heard them from Leigh or his friends. And that had bothered her a bit.

In fact she was thinking absently of them when a knock sounded on her door and Violet, who never asked to be invited in, poked her head around it and said, 'Mrs Sommerville sent me to find you, Mrs Meredith. They're having a pre-party drink in the drawing-room—oh! You're not even ready yet!' She advanced into the room concernedly. She was wearing a figure-hugging bright pink taffeta dress with a raised silver thread pattern on it, and a large orchid pinned to her shoulder.

Meredith blinked. 'Why, Violet, what a lovely orchid,' she said.

Violet beamed. 'I went into Scone last week on my day

off and ordered it,' she confided. 'Just sets my dress off nicely, doesn't it?'

'It does, yes.'

'Mind you, I'm green with envy over your dress!' Violet went on. 'I think it's absolutely super! But is something wrong? Is your leg playing up?'

'No! I'm just being slow,' Meredith replied wryly. Violet never lost an opportunity to comment on her leg, but it was so obviously with concern and the best of intentions, Meredith could never find it in her heart to be annoyed with her persistence. In fact, like Mrs Sommerville, Meredith had come to appreciate that behind Violet's occasionally irritating ways and almost insatiable curiosity there lurked a surprising fund of plain common sense and a rather down-to-earth humanity.

To Evan, though, Violet still remained anathema. A soul like a boiled ham, Meredith had heard him mutter, unoriginally, about Violet once. But the fact remained that she was devoted to his grandmother and did take very great care of her.

'Give me five minutes, Violet,' Meredith said, 'and I'll be there!'

She took nearly twenty in the hope that she might escape the family pre-party drink, and was all but successful.

'There you are, Meredith,' Mrs Sommerville said with some relief. 'I do hope you haven't been working! You've done enough as it is.'

'No, I've been dressing,' Meredith said gaily as she accepted a glass of sherry from Evan, who was looking immaculate but curiously withdrawn in a black dinner-suit with a snowy white shirt front. Black suits his fair hair, she thought, then deliberately cut off her thoughts.

'Well, it was certainly worth waiting for!' Sarah, who

had been working at the winery all day, and had brought her clothes with her, said. 'You look stunning, Meredith!'

'Thank you, Sarah. So do you,' Meredith replied, more than ever conscious of her curiously ambivalent feelings towards Sarah Healey. There was no doubt she could be very nice—Mrs Sommerville had been right. And if Chris was right too in his estimation of Sarah Healey—well, perhaps she had cause to feel possessive of Evan and everything else at Sommerville. Only I wonder if she realises what a complex man Evan Sommerville is? Meredith mused, as she watched them standing side by side, then caught her breath suddenly and turned away. Because Sarah had tilted her face laughingly to Evan, and dressed in a rich ruby gown that complemented her dark hair perfectly, she made a stunning foil for his tall, fair looks.

A moment later, the sort-of-butler personage the catering company had provided appeared with the first of the guests. An hour later the party was in full swing, although Chris hadn't arrived—a fact which was causing Mrs Sommerville some concern.

'Dear Grandmama, Chris is the least punctual person I know,' Meredith heard Evan say to her wryly.

'But this party is special and he knows it!'

'He'll be—in fact, here he is. Well,' Evan said in a rather quizzical tone of voice which caused Meredith who was standing nearby to turn around for some reason. 'I do believe,' he went on, 'that little brother has come up with a winner this time. Someone I seem to vaguely recognise,' he added with a frown.

Meredith stared through the crowd with her lips parted and the feeling that all the blood in her body was draining to her feet. For she at least had no difficulty recognising the girl on Chris's arm.

Oh God, she thought, not Nadia. And he's bringing her

over. She closed her eyes briefly.

But when she opened them, Nadia von Brentlow, clad in ice-blue, was still advancing across the room, Evan was looking suddenly enlightened, Mrs Sommerville delighted and just about everyone of the seventy guests enthralled at who had suddenly appeared in their midst.

Model, writer, traveller, Nadia von Brentlow had taken society by storm some years before and for a while it had been impossible to pick up a magazine without seeing her dynamic and elegantly gaunt features, blonde cropped hair and leggy body displayed within it—clothed, of course, although sometimes minimally so. Then she had disappeared from the fashion scene, only to reappear like Halley's Comet at regular intervals in the press for other exploits, such as driving across a famous Australian desert single-handed, to mention the most daring. She had written a book about that. Chaining herself to bulldozers about to ravage rain forests was another of her favourite activities— she was, Meredith knew, genuinely a conservationist at heart. Just as she was, Meredith also knew, a genuinely sometimes mysterious, often intriguing and always exciting woman with still a hint of a foreign accent that came from her parents who had migrated to Australia quite late in life and had, Nadia claimed, White Russian antecedents. Meredith believed that too, just as she believed that Leigh had fallen hopelessly in love with Nadia von Brentlow almost from their first meeting. And that Nadia, with the whole world to pick from, had fallen in love with him.

Terribly unfair, Meredith had thought in her more lucid, rational moments. How can I hope to compete against *her*? But her uppermost feeling from the moment she had realised what had happened had been confusion— miserable, sick confusion. Had Leigh fallen out of love with her because she had failed him and because of *that* been susceptible to someone like Nadia? Or had he never really loved her—in which case, why had he married her?

And why, she asked herself mentally, coming back to the present and watching Chris proudly introducing his spectacular partner to his grandmother, dazedly, has she come here? Doesn't she know they never knew about her and Leigh? Well, obviously, or she wouldn't have come, surely. But she must have told Chris something, and she certainly couldn't have expected me to be here. Could she?

Then Chris was standing in front of her, his dark eyes alight with mischief and laughter and his favourite form of address on his lips. 'Darling Merry, you look sensational! May I introduce you to . . .'

But Nadia interrupted him. 'There is no need, Christian,' she said in her husky voice and with a frown in her blue, blue eyes. 'Meredith and I have already met. This is a surprise,' she added baldly.

'Yes,' Meredith replied. 'How are you Nadia?'

'Well, thank you. We must talk some time. And you?'

'Very well, thank you. Chris, why don't you take Nadia over to the buffet? In a little while we shall be dancing.'

'Shall do, Merry. Fancy you two knowing each other.'

'Yes, fancy that,' Evan said to Meredith as his 'little brother' and Nadia drifted away.

'Is there any reason why I shouldn't know her?' Meredith countered coolly. It was the first time she and Evan had conversed directly for weeks.

'No, no reason,' he said mildly. 'I just thought it odd. I can't say why.' He grimaced. 'As for how Chris has managed to get her in tow, that's another mystery. She must be years older than him.'

'Only two or three.'

'Then you know her well, Meredith?'

'You could say so, Evan. It's going *well*, this party, isn't it?'

Evan stared down at her meditatively, at her smooth bare shoulders and the slight rise and fall of her breasts beneath the yellow and gold silk. Then his gaze skimmed the rest of her body, and came back to rest on her face. Meredith gritted her teeth and looked around pointedly, at Mrs Sommerville, resplendent in lilac and glowing with happiness, and with Violet in discreet attendance; at the shining parquet floor which reflected the light of the sparkling chandelier above at the flowers everywhere, then brought her eyes back defiantly to Evan.

'Yes, it's going well,' he said mildly and with a faint quirk at the corner of his mouth. Then the hired band set up on a dais at the end of the dining-room struck up and he inclined his head slightly. 'Shall we dance? We have before, if you care to recall.'

'No.'

'No, you don't care to or . . .'

'Both,' she said through her teeth. 'I don't care to dance and I don't care to remember.'

'You're still angry with me, Merry.'

'If only you knew,' she whispered, and went to walk away but he put a hand on her elbow.

'So very angry!' Evan marvelled.

'And some more,' she said tautly. 'Please let me go.'

He did with another mocking little bow, and walked straight over to Sarah, who melted into his arms. Nor was that the only time Meredith had to watch them dancing, for it happened quite frequently throughout the night.

Not long afterwards, Nadia claimed her.

'You go and dance with some young hopeful, Christian,' she commanded, rather like a greyhound dismissing a playful puppy. 'Meredith and I have some things to catch up on.'

Chris went obediently but looking wildly speculative.

'Is there somewhere we might not be disturbed, Meredith?'

'I don't think that's necessary, Nadia,' Meredith said quietly.

'I do,' Nadia replied briefly. 'We'll try the verandah and take these to keep out the cold.' She scooped up two champagne cocktails from a passing waiter.

Meredith hesitated, then followed her out through the French windows. 'Nadia——' she began. 'Thank you,' she accepted a glass, 'Nadia . . .'

'Will you let me speak first?'

Meredith stared into her sober blue eyes then turned away abruptly. 'What is there to say? It's all history now.'

'First,' said Nadia after a moment, 'I must tell you that I came here on a whim tonight. I haven't known Christian for long, but I like him. And when he invited me, I was suddenly very curious to see the place where Leigh had grown up, to meet his family. I thought, what harm could it do? They didn't know about me, not even you had known about me.'

Meredith swung back incredulously.

'As soon as I saw your face tonight,' Nadia went on quietly, 'I realised that you *had*. That the assurance Leigh had given me the last time we spoke was false. You see, in a way, I'd even hoped that I might see you tonight. To reassure myself that you were all right.'

'I don't understand,' Meredith said, shaken.

Nadia considered for a moment, then grimaced. 'I can hardly blame you. Perhaps I should start at the beginning.' She took a sip of champagne. 'When Leigh and I discovered what we felt for each other,' she said, very straight, 'I decided to go away. I told him that he was not free and that I was not prepared to simply have an affair with him.'

'Go on having an affair with him, don't you mean?' Meredith said barely audibly.

Nadia's eyes flickered, then resumed their level gaze. 'For your sake, I had hoped you hadn't known that either. But yes, that's true. For a little while it was like a madness that would not be contained. I'm not usually given to that kind of lapse from sanity, though. It took me a little while to get my bearings, I guess. That was when I told him I was going away, that he should take time to consider his position—and you. He was always very concerned about hurting you, you know. Perhaps that is why he fooled himself into thinking you didn't know?'

Meredith winced.

'I'm sorry—that sounded rather brutal.' Nadia looked away over the verandah railing and then seemed to sigh. 'Maybe I *am* being naïve to think we can discuss it,' she murmured.

It was Meredith's turn to consider, which she did after making an abrupt, disclaiming gesture as if to . . . what? she wondered. Dissociate myself from this? Isn't that natural, though—natural to feel angry and that this untimely candour does border on brutality? Does she think it helps to know that Leigh was concerned about hurting me? Or is she just trying to be honest?

She realised suddenly how rigidly she was holding her shoulders and forced herself to relax. 'Sometimes it's hard to be rational and, I suppose, adult about these things,' she said with a twisted little smile. 'You might as well go on.'

Nadia looked at her thoughtfully. 'There's not much to add,' she said at last. 'The day we reached that agreement was the last time I saw Leigh. A few weeks later, in Perth, I was reading a four-day-old Sydney newspaper and there was an account of the accident in it.' It was said quietly and with not much expression, but somehow, an unspoken grief came through more clearly than words might have expressed.

'I'm sorry.' The words escaped Meredith involuntarily.

Nadia didn't reply, but she looked away again. And when she did speak it was to say, 'Would you believe me if I said the same to you?'

'Yes.'

'And more so now that I know you knew. In the circumstances it seems so—futile. Did Leigh tell you?'

'No, I asked him.' Meredith paused. 'I only found out by accident really. Then, I couldn't imagine why I'd been so blind. But eventually I could see how tormented he was, so I told him I knew. It seemed as if it was a great weight off his shoulders.' And for days afterwards, she thought but didn't say, he kept telling me it was up to *me* to decide what should be done, that he felt responsible for me. But I knew we couldn't go on, so I finally said I would go away to my aunt in New Zealand. That was the last conversation *we* had.

'It didn't . . . it wasn't the cause of the accident? A row, perhaps?' asked Nadia, Meredith thought fearfully.

'No. Oh no.' It had been a very civilised conversation, actually. 'No, the other party was in the wrong. We never had a chance.'

'Thank God for that—if you know what I mean.'

Meredith nodded slowly. Then she took a deep breath, 'There's something I have to tell you, Nadia. Our marriage was on the rocks, really, before Leigh met you. It wouldn't have survived anyway, probably.'

Nadia studied her in thoughtful silence. 'You knew this at the time?' she said finally.

'No, not really,' Meredith answered honestly. 'At the time I felt desperately hurt and betrayed and alone—

confused.' She broke off and bit her lip.

Nadia waited patiently.

'But now I can't help wondering where it all went,' Meredith said huskily. 'If that makes any sense to you.' She stopped abruptly, and thought, *can't* you?

'Go on,' Nadia prompted curiously.

'Perhaps it's as they say—that truth is the daughter of time,' Meredith went on with an effort. 'That it was only an infatuation. Or perhaps it was finally being able to understand Leigh. I do think now,' she looked up suddenly, straight into Nadia's eyes, 'that he married me on a whim. I was a virgin and determined to stay one. I was a little different from all the other girls he knew. He,' she lifted her shoulders, 'was like that. Given to whims. You two, and I don't mean to be derogatory, but you two would have been much better suited.'

Nadia shrugged and half smiled as if to say *touché*, but not as if she had taken offence, and they stood together for a time in companionable silence. How strange, Meredith thought. But Nadia's next words jolted her.

'And you never told the Sommervilles about Leigh's infidelity? That he had treated you so shabbily? Marrying you on a whim in order to sleep with you, in other words, and then was prepared to discard you?'

Meredith cast the other girl a startled look.

'Ah,' Nadia said in reply to that look, '*I* never believed that other old one about love being blind. I know also that Leigh had his faults. In fact I think it *was* his quixotic character that I loved most. I felt I would never be able to smother him—which is a problem I have had with some of the men in my life. But to get back to the Sommervilles.'

'No, I never told them,' said Meredith. 'And to this day I don't know if I did the right thing, but it was a peculiar situation. For quite some time I wasn't capable of telling anyone anything. Then when I was, Leigh's grandmother had almost adopted me and been so very good to me.' She stopped and sighed. 'It seemed to me that to tell her would have meant destroying some of her illusions about Leigh. I thought there was no point except to make *me* feel less of a fraud. But I haven't touched his money except for medical expenses. I got a fairly substantial compensation for the accident finally.'

Nadia stirred. 'I think you did the right thing. I also think you're entitled to his money. I never for one moment felt that I was. Tell me, are you happy?' she asked abruptly. 'It's been quite a long time now.'

Meredith smiled faintly. 'If I'm not, it isn't your fault or Leigh's. Are you?'

Nadia raised her eyebrows and said softly, 'You've grown up, Meredith. Twenty-two now? Yes,' she said as Meredith nodded, 'but that's not so old. The thing is, when life hits one as it did you, you either grow up quickly or you grow small. One day you will make some man a good wife. You know,' she went on without giving Meredith a chance to say anything, 'Christian asked me to stay the night, but I think that would be wrong now. I'll go back with some friends I've seen. What do you think?'

'I think—yes. But I'm glad you came, Nadia.'

'So am I. Can I give you one piece of advice? Do you think I am qualified to do that? No, don't answer. I will anyway—don't sell yourself short. Your mistakes were the ones of youth—but men seem to think they are the only ones entitled to make them.'

'How?' The word was torn unwittingly from Meredith.

Nadia made a curiously European gesture with her long, slender fingers. 'How did I know? I didn't, although I know you think now it was a great mistake to marry Leigh. But, while you were quite lovely then, you are unusually beautiful now, with a hint of . . . how can I put it? Tragedy, ice, strength, reserve, yes. And some man will find that irresistible but will probably make your life hell in the process until he is convinced he can break it all down. Men are like that too, I've discovered. And talking of such, here comes my little friend Christian, positively bursting with curiosity. *Au revoir*, Meredith.'

'*Au revoir*,' Meredith answered, but some moments later.

She thought, throughout the rest of the evening, that no one would be able to tell what a momentous evening it had been for her. She thought that it was one of the better performances of her life. Evan certainly went out of his way to ignore her and to concentrate on Sarah, for which she thought she was grateful. And Mrs Sommerville was so happy and excited, so in her element after the long painful weeks she had endured, nothing seemed capable of denting it. Not even the discovery that Violet—fortress Violet— had a chink in her armour; champagne cocktails, which not only made her tipsy but distinctly flirtatious. It had been Meredith who had spotted the problem and taken her away to be sobered up by Mrs Whittington.

'Was I very dreadful?' Violet enquired, returning to the party, looking pale but composed.

'Oh no,' Meredith replied not quite truthfully and restraining a smile. 'But why don't you go to bed? I mean if you're feeling unwell?'

'Because I've got a job to do and do it I shall.'

'I can help Mrs Sommerville to bed, Violet.'

Violet set her jaw. 'Now I know how strong those nasty drinks are, I won't be touching another drop, Mrs Meredith, rest assured!'

But, Meredith discovered later, she had left Chris out of her calculations. After the last guests had left, Meredith had changed and set to work to help Mrs Whittington put the house to bed. It was not in Mrs Whittington's nature to leave it until the morning. 'At least it will be tidy,' she had said. 'Can't stand getting up to untidiness.'

Even after Mrs Whittington had departed to bed, though, Meredith thought she might not be able to sleep, so she brewed herself a cup of tea and sat at the long kitchen table staring at it. That was how Chris found her.

'I thought everyone was asleep,' she said, glancing up at him as he came through the hall door, still wearing his frilled shirt and dark trousers but a sweater instead of his jacket and tie.

'Then why aren't you?' he asked.

'I was just helping Mrs Whittington.'

'Thought so. I knocked on your door. I want to talk to you, Meredith,' he said abruptly, his dark eyes sober and concerned.

A flickering premonition touched Meredith. But surely Nadia wouldn't have told him, she thought. 'Well, it's a little late, Chris,' she said, striving for a casual note. 'Can't it wait until morning?'

'No, it can't,' he said intently, then his eyes lit on the teapot and he turned around to get himself a cup from the huge old dresser. 'I had no idea,' he went on, sitting down opposite her.

'Of what?' she said steadily, and poured milk and then tea into his cup.

'Of Nadia and Leigh!'

Meredith set the teapot down carefully. 'Did she tell you?' she asked eventually.

'No! But I sensed that she'd changed almost from the moment she arrived. She . . .'

'Who did, then?' Meredith interrupted.

'Lavinia Marsh,' Chris said impatiently. 'She asked me if

I'd taken up where Leigh had left off—I thought she meant *you* at first. But she went on to explain.'

'I don't think I know her,' Meredith broke in again.

'You mightn't. She was the one in the hideous black and white and purple outfit. Her father's some big shot in the Electricity Commission and we've known each other, the families at any rate, for ages. I once suspected *she* had a crush on Leigh—but that's not the point!' He eyed Meredith frustratedly. 'She was right, wasn't she? About Nadia and Leigh. It all makes *sense* now.'

Meredith fiddled with the sugar basin. 'Chris, I'd much rather you forgot about all this. Leigh . . .' She hesitated.

'Is dead. I know,' said Chris. 'And you've been very loyal to his memory, Merry. But at great expense to yourself.' He looked at her keenly.

'That's nonsense,' Meredith said sharply. 'It would have helped no one to know.'

'What about Evan?' Chris shot at her.

She blinked. 'What about him?'

'Don't tell me he hasn't made your life hell one way or another since Leigh died, Merry,' Chris said quietly, 'I've said before, I'm not blind.'

'I *told* you why, Chris.'

'But don't you think even dear Evan would find it hard to be so sanctimonious if he knew *Leigh* had been glaringly unfaithful to *you*? Had been conducting a blazing affair apparently with—and even if you water Lavinia's gossip down by about fifty per cent, which it's normally wise to do—apparently with not much concern for who knew. Was that what you had, by the way?' he added swiftly.

'What do you mean?'

'This . . . peccadillo of yours that Evan discovered? Was it a blazing affair?'

'I . . . no, but, Chris . . .'

'I thought not. Did it happen after you knew about Leigh and Nadia? You did know about it, didn't you?'

'Yes, I did, but . . .'

'Afterwards, then?'

'Chris—*yes*! But what difference does it make? Look, this is making *me* a little angry,' Meredith said tightly, and went to get up.

'Sit down, Merry,' Chris said softly but with a look so surprisingly like one of Evan's more autocratic ones, she sat back out of sheer surprise and would have been moved to laugh in other circumstances. 'You know, Merry, it would have been quite human to say to yourself then—well, what's sauce for the gander is sauce for the goose.'

Meredith stared at him and for the life of her couldn't help her expression softening into one of exasperated affection. She said, 'No, it would not. Chris, I don't know why you persist in taking this—indulgent view of what happened, although I'm grateful, I really am but . . .'

'I told you once before how fond I was of you,' Chris said imperturbably. 'I also pride myself on reading characters. Yours, the one you've given yourself anyway, just doesn't seem to fit. Okay, if we rule out the goose and gander bit, what's next?'

'Are you ticking all this off from a mental list?' she enquired acidly. 'Or just playing Sherlock Holmes?'

He laughed. 'Well, if I were, I'd suggest then that you were hurt and lonely and confused and some *man* offered you—a little warmth, maybe. How does that read?'

Meredith closed her eyes. 'Please,' she said, 'don't go on.'

'Ah, gold,' Chris murmured, then he said abruptly, 'I could put it to Evan for you. I'm sure he'd understand that. He's not really such a bad bloke underneath, and now that I know Nadia I have the perfect excuse.'

'*No!*' Meredith's eyes flew open.

'Why not?'

'Because it wouldn't be fair to Nadia.'

'If you ask me, she was very concerned about *you*. Trust me, Merry. And the other thing is, Evan knew Leigh was no saint. We all did.'

'Chris,' Meredith whispered, and rubbed her face agitatedly, 'Chris, there's something *you* don't understand.'

'I don't? Tell me,' he invited.

She stared at him helplessly and licked her lips. 'It wasn't just ... some man.'

'What do you mean?'

'It ... it was Evan himself.'

CHAPTER FIVE

'EVAN?' Chris's voice cracked with surprise and he said his brother's name again.

'Yes, Evan,' Meredith retorted, then bit her lip.

'You're right, I don't understand,' Chris said in almost comical bewilderment then.

Meredith stood up and began to clear away the teacups, both cold now and untasted. 'He didn't know who I was and vice versa. *Now* do you see that there's nothing you could do? In fact you can only make things worse.'

But Chris was sitting back frowning abstractedly as if he hadn't even heard the last part of what she'd said. 'Well, I never,' he said presently. 'I must say I didn't expect that. But of course I should have.'

'Chris.' Meredith looked at him nervously, wishing now that she hadn't told him. Why on earth did I? she asked herself. Because I've got the horrible feeling that Christian Sommerville is not only very perceptive but unusually tenacious. And to her horror she felt sudden tears brimmimg.

'Oh, Merry,' Chris said anxiously, bounding up with a look of concern, 'don't cry!'

'I'm not,' she muttered, and blinked.

'Yes, you are!' He came round the table and put his arms round her lightly.

For a second she hesitated, then, she rested her forehead wearily on his shoulder. 'Please promise me you'll forget all about this, Chris.'

The more
you love romance . . .
the more
you'll love this offer

FREE!

Mail this heart today! (See inside)

Join us on a Harlequin Honeymoon
and we'll give you
4 free books
A free makeup mirror and brush kit
And a free mystery gift

IT'S A
HARLEQUIN HONEYMOON—
A SWEETHEART
OF A FREE OFFER!
HERE'S WHAT YOU GET:

1. **Four New Harlequin Presents® Novels—FREE!**

   Take a Harlequin Honeymoon with your four exciting romances—yours FREE from Harlequin Reader Service. Each of these hot-off-the-press novels brings you the passion and tenderness of today's greatest love stories...your free passports to bright new worlds of love and foreign adventure.

2. **A Lighted Makeup Mirror and Brush Kit—FREE!**

   This lighted makeup mirror and brush kit allows plenty of light for those quick touch-ups. It operates on two easy-to-replace batteries and bulbs (batteries not included). It holds everything you need for a perfect finished look yet is small enough to slip into your purse or pocket—4-⅛″ x 3″ closed.

3. **An Exciting Mystery Bonus—FREE!**

   You'll be thrilled with this surprise gift. It is a useful and attractive item and will be the source of many compliments.

4. **Money-Saving Home Delivery!**

   Join Harlequin Reader Service and enjoy the convenience of previewing eight new books every month delivered right to your home. Each book is yours for only $2.24—26¢ less per book than what you pay in stores—plus 89¢ postage and handling per shipment. Great savings plus total convenience add up to a sweetheart of a deal for you!

5. **More Surprise Gifts**

   Because our home subscribers are our most valued readers, we'll be sending you additional free gifts from time to time—as a token of our appreciation.

START YOUR HARLEQUIN HONEYMOON TODAY—JUST
COMPLETE, DETACH AND MAIL YOUR FREE-OFFER CARD

Get your fabulous gifts ABSOLUTELY FREE!

MAIL THIS CARD TODAY.

DETACH AND MAIL TODAY!

GIVE YOUR HEART TO HARLEQUIN

YES! Please send me my four Harlequin Presents novels FREE, along with my free lighted makeup mirror and brush kit and free mystery gift as explained on the opposite page.

NAME _____
(PLEASE PRINT)

ADDRESS _____ APT. _____

CITY _____ PROV. _____

POSTAL CODE _____ 308 CIH U1CJ

PRICES SUBJECT TO CHANGE. OFFER LIMITED TO ONE PER HOUSEHOLD AND NOT VALID TO PRESENT SUBSCRIBERS.

PLACE HEART STICKER HERE

HARLEQUIN READER SERVICE "NO RISK" GUARANTEE
— There's no obligation to buy—and the free books and gifts remain yours to keep.
— You pay the lowest price possible and receive books before they appear in stores.
— You may end your subscription anytime—just write and let us know.

PRINTED IN U.S.A.

START YOUR
HARLEQUIN HONEYMOON TODAY.
JUST COMPLETE, DETACH AND MAIL YOUR
FREE OFFER CARD.

If offer card below is missing, write to: Harlequin Reader Service, P.O. Box 609
Fort Erie, Ontario L2A 5X3

**Business
Reply Mail**

No Postage Stamp
Necessary if Mailed
in Canada

Postage will be paid by

Harlequin Reader Service®
P.O. Box 609
Fort Erie, Ontario
L2A 9Z9

Canada Post
Postes Canada
125

DETACH AND MAIL TODAY!

'But how . . .'

'*Please*, Chris,' she begged, and stiffened suddenly as the hall door clicked open. She jerked her head around and for the second time felt the blood drain to her feet.

It was Evan standing in the doorway.

'Well, well,' he drawled after a pause so laden with tension you could have cut it with a knife, 'you are running true to form, Meredith. As for you, Chris,' he added but with his eyes still on Meredith's white face, '*you* are flying high these days, aren't you? But if the ladies are willing, why not?' He shrugged. 'Goodnight then, young lovers,' he murmured carelessly, but the look in his eyes was quite different. Meredith felt scorched by it.

She sagged against Chris as the door closed and whispered, 'Oh God!' Then she stiffened again and said in a different tone of voice, 'Chris, what are you doing?'

But she didn't need to be told, for it was obvious Chris was laughing heartily but quite silently.

She pulled herself away angrily. 'If you think it's funny, I don't,' she said with barely suppressed violence.

'Well, Merry, I have to confess I do,' he admitted, and leant across to kiss her cheek.

She moved away restlessly and said bitterly, 'You're impossible, Chris.'

'So it would seem,' he murmured, still grinning.

'But if,' she said through her teeth, 'you don't forget about all this, I shall . . .'

'Rest assured you're in no danger from me,' he said earnestly. 'Cross my heart and hope to die. Do you know,' he added ingenuously, 'Evan wasn't so far off the mark either.'

Meredith opened her mouth to speak, but shut it and simply stared at him.

'I mean,' he elucidated, 'the thought had crossed my mind to be very attracted to you, but the thing is, I like you too much. Which means to say I'd rather have you as a sister. Does that offend you?'

Meredith shook her head, but not to say no—only to acquaint herself with this bewildering twist. 'Offend me?' she repeated somewhat dazedly. 'No, I'd rather you liked me, actually. But—do you mean you *can't* . . . like the girls you fall in love with?'

'It's hard.'

'It shouldn't be, surely?'

'I find it is. And, for example, do you like Evan?'

She caught her breath.

'Point made,' he said wryly.

'Chris . . .'

But he said gently, 'Bedtime, I think. That secret is safe with me too, by the way. Goodnight, Merry.'

'*Chris* . . .'

But he had gone, and Meredith was left staring at the door.

The moon is blue, she thought, standing at her bedroom window a few minutes later. Again. It was a blue moon the first time I met Evan. She pulled the curtains closed abruptly and changed into her nightgown.

The moon is never blue, she told herself light-headedly as she got into bed. It just sometimes looks a bluey-white, often in fact, and its colour bears no relation to the crises in my life whatsoever. And I'm overtired.

But sleep refused to come because her mind was alive with old images—so many of them resurrected tonight. And particularly, the one she most wanted to forget. But Chris's words had brought it back so clearly, some man offering you a little warmth.

Had it been only that? she thought for perhaps the millionth time as she lay quiet and still in the vast soft bed. Or was it only evidence of my fickle nature? Because how could you be in love with two men at the same time, how could you respond like that to any man when you'd only just met him—hadn't even been introduced?

She closed her eyes and felt herself slipping back in time to, of all things, a masked fancy dress ball. I don't want to go—why is Leigh so insistent? Well, you know why, don't you, Meredith? Because Nadia—another N, Nuriootpa, Nunawadding, Nhulunbuy and now Nadia, is that fate?— will be there. Tears clouded her hazel eyes and every instinct she possessed rose up to scream at Leigh—how can you *do* this to me? How can you imagine I'd be so blind as not to *know* what you feel for her even without that shabby little bit of incontrovertible proof?

But she didn't. She gave in and wore the costume of his choosing—a sort of medieval court-lady outfit in brown velvet and cream taffeta with gold-thread embroidery and lacing. She discarded the tall pointed hat and chose the alternative headgear that came with the costume, a gold-netted snood through which her hair gleamed gold too. And she stood in front of the mirror while Leigh was happily donning his court costume, and tried to pull the rather revealing and tight bodice of the dress up a bit so that the creamy swell of her breasts wasn't quite so exposed. Then she pulled on the brown half-gloves, and with sudden gratitude, put on her mask.

For which Leigh teased her on the hour-long drive to Richmond, but all she said was that she might as well get used to it.

The ball was being held in an ancient, beautiful redbrick

pile on the Hawkesbury River, which seemed to be overflowing with guests even as they arrived, and she wasn't sure who the host was because apart from the masks and fancy dresses, he was a friend of Leigh's she had never met. And there seemed to be only one rule to this party—no removing of masks until midnight!

'That makes it much more fun!' Meredith heard a bewigged Madame Pompadour say excitedly. 'Just imagine the indiscretions one could commit!'

'Ah, but all will be revealed at midnight, don't forget,' someone had answered her laughingly.

All the same, Meredith had recognised Nadia almost immediately. She had come as the Queen of Hearts, but her slight accent and distinctive phraseology was unmistakable—at least to me it is, Meredith thought, but then I seem to be developing a sixth sense about Nadia von Brentlow. She had turned away, sick at heart, because the almost tangible magnetism that seemed to flow between the Queen of Hearts and a certain court gentleman was not lost on her either.

What she hadn't anticipated was that her courage or whatever it was would run out so abruptly halfway through the evening so that she had to make the excuse to Leigh that she had a headache, and then parry his concern—surely it couldn't be genuine?—by saying that all she needed was some fresh air and she wouldn't dream of letting him go with her. And anyway, she'd be paying a visit to the ladies', too.

He didn't persist, but instead of looking for a cloakroom, she found a dim side-verandah that was deserted, and with a sigh of relief, stripped off her mask and stared out to see a blue moon sailing high above some silver clouds and trailing a path of silver on the quiet waters of the river.

Then a tall shadow detached itself from a pillar, and she realised suddenly that she wasn't alone. What appeared to be a monk in a long brown habit complete with hood was standing only a few paces from her.

'Oh, sorry,' she said wearily, 'I didn't see you.'

'That's all right,' the monk answered. 'I don't have a monopoly on this verandah. Party getting a bit much for you?'

'Yes,' she confessed, and added baldly, a little to her surprise, 'If you must know, I think this kind of thing is a bit silly. Grown-up people going around masked and so on.'

The monk slipped off his hood and mask and the moonlight revealed thick fair hair and glinted into his eyes so that they looked silver, like the river. 'Actually, I agree with you.'

'Then why did you come?' she asked. 'Did someone make you?'

The man grinned faintly. 'Is that what happened to you? No, no one made me. It was all my own mistake, but I should have known better because our host is rather a good friend of mine and every party he's ever given has been a bit of a bash. He forgets who he's invited. He even forgot to tell me it was fancy-dress—this,' he gestured down at the brown habit, 'is his. He ordered three outfits to give himself plenty to choose from. Are you on your own?'

Meredith grimaced. 'You could say so.'

'How come?'

She hesitated. 'Only . . . because I feel like being on my own,' she said finally.

'That sounds rather mysterious—is it meant to be Maid Marian?'

Meredith looked down at her costume and laughed. 'I'm not sure *what* it's meant to be!'

'It's very fetching. I wonder—perhaps I'm meant to be Friar Tuck!'

She giggled. 'Oh no,' she said, 'not you!'

'Why not?'

'Well, I've always thought of Friar Tuck as short and fat and with a bald pate—quite the opposite from you.'

'Why, thank you,' her companion said with a lazy, devastatingly attractive smile, she realised suddenly. 'May I return the compliment? I'm sure Maid Marian was never as lovely as you.'

Meredith swallowed suddenly and stared up into those silvery grey eyes. He was, she judged, several years older than Leigh and it wasn't only his smile that was attractive, she found herself thinking rather dazedly, but the lines of his tall body which the habit seemed to reveal rather than conceal. A little tremor ran down her spine, as she looked away in some confusion.

But if he guessed her confusion, all he said was, 'Have you eaten?'

'No, not yet.'

'Would you like to? Out here? There's a table over there. I could get something from the buffet.'

She turned back doubtfully. 'Are you . . . I mean, on your own?'

'Yes. Or I could escort you back inside, if you preferred, Maid Marian,' he said softly. 'It's up to you.'

'I . . .' Meredith bit her lip and visualised going back inside to Leigh and the Queen of Hearts. 'No, I think I'd rather stay out here.' Let him come and find *me*, she thought dismally, if he can tear himself away.

'I'll be right back,' her monk said, putting on his mask and adjusting his cowl.

He was too, in an astonishingly short time, bearing two

plates and two tall wine glasses which he set down on the wrought-iron table, then he drew up two chairs and held hers politely for her to sit down.

But before he sat down himself, he rummaged through the apparently capacious pockets of the habit and produced knives and forks, a salt cellar, and from the other side, a bottle of wine. 'I always wondered where monks put all their possessions. Now I know.'

'Do monks have possessions?' she asked with a grin.

'Well, that's a point.' He sat down. 'They must, but of course only unworldly ones. Damn!'

'What?'

'The wine is open as you see, and I'm a bit damp down one side as you can't see. Never mind,' he poured out some wine and lifted his glass, 'what shall we toast? By the way, I got you a bit of everything—I hope you're hungry!'

Meredith looked down at her plate, laden with cold chicken, smoked salmon, delicious-looking thick pink ham and succulent salad, and decided, surprisedly, that she was. She picked up her glass. 'I am now, and I've thought of the perfect toast.'

'Oh?' Those grey eyes quizzed her amusedly.

'Definitely—to Sherwood Forest, of course! Although I'm sure they never ate so well there.'

'To Sherwood Forest!' her companion echoed solemnly, then he smiled faintly. 'What a pity I didn't come as Robin Hood.'

Meredith looked away and said the first thing that came into her head. 'Does the moon look blue to you?' He glanced up. 'Oh, don't answer that,' she said hastily. 'It's just one of my silly fancies.'

'Well, it does, perhaps. Are you prone to silly fancies?'

She had to laugh. She said with a touch of irony, 'Thanks. No, not really.' Somehow that seemed to tide them over an awkward moment and they talked easily, although she could never remember what about afterwards, as they ate. He refilled her wine glass, and after a while they fell into a companionable silence until he raised his glass to her, and said, 'They're playing your tune. Would you like to dance?'

She frowned and concentrated and realised that the slow, plaintive notes of *Blue Moon* were wafting out to them. 'Out here?' she said uncertainly, when she should have said just no, she thought.

His lips moved in a slow, chiselled smile. 'It's nicer out here. Not so crowded.'

'All right.'

If they'd been made for each other, they couldn't have been better suited as dancing partners—the shocking thought crossed Meredith's mind and caused her to make a small, inarticulate sound in her throat.

'What is it?'

'N-nothing,' she stammered, and out of despair, perhaps, laid her cheek on his shoulder. 'I mean,' she whispered, 'I don't even know you.'

'Does it worry you?' He held her slender body even closer.

'Yes. No, I don't know why. But you seem awfully nice.' Do I mean *nice* or . . . no, surely not, she thought, as she felt him laugh silently.

She lifted her head and stared up at him, her mouth trembling suddenly, her eyes dark and wide.

'So do you,' he murmured, his lips barely moving and with his lids half lowered over the silver grey of his eyes. In an instant before he did it, she knew he was going to kiss her—she couldn't even console herself later with the knowledge that she hadn't *known*. Because she had. And had been unable or unwilling to resist.

It was a long, slow kiss, and such was the drugging power of his lips, and his hands moving slowly on the curve of her back, that when he lifted his head at last, she whispered involuntarily, 'Don't.'

'Don't?'

'Don't stop. Oh God . . .' She closed her eyes and felt a tide of colour flood her cheeks.

But he only laughed silently again and hugged her gently, and kissed the top of her head. 'I'd much rather not,' he said, releasing her but taking her hand and leading her over to the balustrade. 'Only you're right, perhaps it is time we met. I'm . . .'

But Meredith clenched his hand suddenly and then pulled free to turn away.

'What's wrong?' he asked after a moment, and took her shoulders to turn her back gently. And he raised his eyebrows at her expression of sheer confusion. 'So lovely,' he marvelled, and touched her cheek, 'but very young, I think. Twenty?'

'Nearly.'

He smiled. 'And very troubled suddenly. Why, I wonder?'

'This hasn't ever happened to me before.'

'That's interesting,' he said after a moment, his eyes suddenly acute and probing. 'It hasn't to me, either. Not quite so . . . out of a blue moon, shall we say. So we're in the same boat, my Maid Marian.'

Meredith swallowed and licked her lips and opened her mouth to say she knew not what, to beg him not to look at her like that, perhaps, with those grey eyes amused but also with something much more serious in their depths, to tell him the awful truth about herself, possibly. But Leigh chose that moment to erupt on to the verandah.

'My God, Meredith,' he said incredulously, 'where the hell have you been? I was just about to send out search parties. And to complicate matters, there's someone in a nearly identical outfit—she even had me fooled for a while. What the devil? *Evan*? Is that you?' Leigh's voice rose with supreme surprise and he snatched off his own mask, as if to see better without it.

'Well, well,' the man he had called Evan drawled, and belatedly, the implication of that name hit Meredith, so that her mouth fell open and she went white, 'if it isn't you, brother Leigh!'

'I didn't know you were here—of course it's me!' Leigh retorted a shade belligerently. 'These bloody masks, I'm beginning to think it was a damn fool idea. So,' he seemed to force himself to relax, and went on, 'well, you've met Meredith, obviously. That's quite an honour, Bro, because you're the first of the family to do so.'

Much as she wanted to, Meredith found she couldn't tear her eyes from Leigh's brother's face. And she saw the way his grey eyes narrowed, saw his long, strong hand move abruptly on the balustrade, she saw everything fall into place in his mind, and then she closed her eyes, because she suddenly couldn't bear to see any more.

'Are you telling me, Leigh,' Evan's voice was quiet and ominously silky, 'that this is the wife you saw fit to take so secretively, and insisted on keeping—hidden?'

'Evan,' said Leigh in a curiously tight-lipped way, 'I've told you before, I make my own decisions now, and being head of the family doesn't entitle you to have any say in my life.'

'Oh? When have I done that?'

'Every time you make me feel like an idle playboy,' Leigh grated. 'Because what *I'm* good at doesn't earn a fast buck you seem to think it's somehow contemptible. But let me tell you . . .'

'Don't bother,' Evan interrupted, Meredith thought wearily. 'So long as I make sure the fast bucks keep coming in, it's all right, isn't it?'

'Oh, come on! There's millions of them!' Leigh said contemptuously. 'And anyway, that's what *you* like doing. You know, Merry could never understand why I hadn't taken her to meet you—now she might!'

Evan Sommerville turned towards Meredith. 'Merry,' he said in a dangerously quiet, contemplative voice, as if trying the name for size. He smiled suddenly, but it didn't reach his eyes. 'Well, Maid Marian, I don't suppose I'll ever forget you, even if Leigh does see fit to whisk you back into hiding.'

'Now look here, Evan, there's no point in taking our differences out on Merry, and anyway, I was planning to take her to see Gran soon.'

'Oh, I had no intention of taking anything out on your lovely *wife*, Leigh,' Evan said casually but with an underlying chill in his voice that made Meredith cringe inwardly. 'In fact I wish you all the happiness in the world. I really thought she was the picture of . . . young innocence. You see, we hadn't in fact met—rather been introduced. She was just telling me about all the things that had never happened to her. Weren't you, ma'am?'

Could Leigh detect the irony in that quiet casual voice? Meredith wondered dimly as she followed Evan's grey gaze which flickered down to her hands in their unrevealing half-gloves, then came back to rest on her still white, dazed face.

'Yes,' she whispered, and for some reason straightened her shoulders almost defiantly. Was it an inkling she'd had, she often wondered later, of how cruel Evan Sommerville could be, that had made her make that gesture? And lift her chin too? Only, with the benefit of hindsight of course, she had later realised how it had consolidated Evan's view of her. And, as she had asked herself countless times afterwards, could she blame him? No, only herself for half an hour of sheer madness and then defiance on top of it. But it hadn't really been defiance. It had been acceptance ... and numbness and horror. Or like saying, am I all the things you think I am? What other excuse could there be, perhaps I am.

Then Leigh had led her away but not, incredibly, because he understood the cause of that almost electric air of friction between *her* and his brother Evan, as he demonstrated by saying to her—don't let him get to you on my account, Merry. I can hold my own!

That was when tears had sparkled in her eyes suddenly, and he had laughed and hugged her and told her she was more loyal than he deserved. Then he had gone suddenly quiet and rather abruptly suggested they go home. And once home, he had taken her in his arms and made love to her the way he used to, and her confused, battered heart had taken refuge in this act, while in her mind she had deliberately blocked out Evan Sommerville and Nadia von Brentlow.

But her hopes, and curiously Evan's obvious contempt for Leigh had made her feel oddly protective and think she was *really* in love with him, were soon dashed.

Nadia still seemed to be everywhere they went, and Leigh even more obviously like a moth attracted to a flame, while Meredith reminded herself of an ostrich. But what else am I to do? she asked herself time and time again. I can only hope that this thing will burn itself out.

Then Leigh got a note from Mrs Sommerville, saying that she was in Sydney and would he *please* bring Meredith to meet her.

'Evan's doing,' Leigh said grimly. 'Very well, we will.'

'Leigh . . .' Meredith began.

'Oh, you don't have to be frightened of my grandmother, Merry. She's a honey. Actually I would have taken you to meet her after our wedding, but she was overseas. Well,' he shrugged, 'I guess I've made my point, so we'll go.'

Meredith stared at him, not knowing whether to be happy, frightened stiff of what Evan might have told Mrs Sommerville about her, or just plain confused. Would Leigh want to take her to meet his grandmother if he was thinking of leaving her for Nadia?

And yet, even in this almost paralytic state, she couldn't help but be charmed by Mrs Sommerville, and after deciding that Evan couldn't possibly have told his grandmother about what had happened, found herself relaxing a little. Leigh had left them alone for a while, during which time Mrs Sommerville had chatted about the family and said quite openly that in spite of some rather basic differences between them, they *had* been very close as boys; said again how lovely she thought Meredith was and how lucky Leigh was; and with the utmost delicacy tried to find out whether there was any chance of her becoming a great-grandmother soon—something she was really looking forward to, she had indicated.

Perhaps it was the strain of this visit, or perhaps it was the culmination of months of strain or just sheer desperation, Meredith never really knew, but on the way home, she quite suddenly put her cards on the table in a curious way.

'Leigh, I want to have a baby.'

Did I say that? she wondered as the words seemed to echo round the car, and she saw Leigh's hands tighten on the steering-wheel.

'No,' he said eventually and definitely with a white shade around his mouth.

'Why not?' she whispered.

'We haven't even been married for twelve months, Meredith!' he said explosively then. 'What's this almighty rush?'

'But it's not that, is it, Leigh?' she flashed at him, finding herself breathlessly angry all of a sudden. At least he could be *honest* with me, she told herself, forgetting for a moment how she had dreaded this moment of truth. 'It's because you don't love me any more—I wonder if you ever did? Not the way you've fallen in love with Nadia von Brentlow, anyway,' she said bitterly, and turned a set, pale face towards him to see his reaction.

It told her everything she hadn't wanted to know, and more, as succeeding expressions chased across Leigh's handsome face. Incredulity at first, as if to say—how did *you* know, then guilt and something rather distraught and unusually strained. But finally, relief.

And that was when she got her first intimation, like a small quiet thought in the midst of mental chaos, that Leigh Sommerville was something of an emotional coward. But for reasons it took her a long time to fathom, she refused to let that thought take root. Even when, over the next week, *he* obstinately refused to come to a decision himself and kept saying to her—it's up to you, Merry. I married you and I feel responsible for you. Whatever you want to do, we'll do.

Which they never did decide, because at the end of that week, he was dead.

And I, Meredith thought, years later, lying in her bed at Sommerville after the party, was left as if still suspended in that emotional maelstrom. If only I'd understood at the time that that was his way of letting himself off the hook instead of blindly ignoring that small voice and thinking he was being quite noble—I might have saved myself a lot of suffering. And ... I wonder if Nadia did honestly realise what I've thought for a long time but really come to *know* finally, tonight. That it was quite a basic character flaw in Leigh's make-up, I think. More than being charmingly quixotic. But of course she doesn't know that he—at least pretended, that he felt it his duty to stay with me if I'd wanted it? Not that I could ever tell her. But if she did, she must have loved him very much, and perhaps *she* might have been the one to inspire a deep commitment from him.

But even if I've finally solved Leigh, tonight, there's still Evan, she reflected, and twisted restlessly, only to gasp slightly as a flicker of pain shot down her leg.

'Damn!' she muttered. 'Have I been overdoing it?'

But the pain subsided and she was left in peace to confront the mental picture she had of Evan's scorching grey glance and his instinctive reading of the little tableau she and Chris had made.

She only fell asleep when the eastern sky was beginning to lighten at the edges.

When she woke up it was after ten and raining heavily, and her leg was locked solid—or so it felt. She lay back and tried to relax it and tentatively started the exercises that would gradually loosen the muscles and tendons the accident had damaged, but to no avail. And it was a pale, haggard face she turned to the door at the sound of a knock, to call 'come in' unsteadily.

It was Chris.

'Merry,' he said, just poking his head around the door, 'are you decent? Did I wake you? Sorry, but I'm leaving now and I thought we ought to ... Merry?' His tone sharpened, and he stepped in to the room.

'Chris, could you ask Violet to come and help me?' she whispered.

He stared at her, then turned away hastily and she could hear him calling for Violet imperatively as he strode down the passage.

She closed her eyes and grimaced. And as she'd expected, it was not only Violet who came but Mrs Sommerville and Mrs Whittington—even Sarah Healey, although there was no sign of Evan.

'What is it?' The question was asked three times before Violet arrived, all in tones of distinct anxiety, but before she got a chance to explain, Violet did arrive and she didn't need to have anything explained to her. To Meredith's relief, she took immediate command and shooed everyone else out.

'Now what have you been doing, Mrs Meredith?' she demanded, and narrowed her eyes. 'Quite a lot of dancing last night and generally quite a lot of rushing around lately—you've been doing too much!' she scolded as she swept the bedclothes aside. 'You forget that these muscles often need years to be as strong as they once were.'

'It's been years, Violet,' Meredith said, close to tears.

Violet snorted. 'Two years, you told me, didn't you? That's chicken feed. Now,' she added in a slightly less hectoring tone, 'I'm going to get Mrs Sommerville's heating pad and when we've warmed you up a bit, I'll massage it. Don't go away.'

It took over an hour of Violet's ministrations before Meredith was mobile and able to walk around the room unaided.

'I'll be fine now,' she said.

'You'll go back to bed, Mrs Meredith,' Violet commanded.

'But Violet, that's the last thing I need!'

'Not today, it isn't. The doctor's coming up to see you. Have a shower and I'll get out a fresh nightgown.'

'Violet!' Meredith exclaimed angrily. 'You know that's not necessary. Why did you do it?'

'I don't know it's not necessary,' Violet countered. 'But actually, I didn't do it. Mr Sommerville rang for him.'

'Chris? But why didn't you . . .'

'Not that Mr Sommerville, the other one, and what he says goes around here, in case you hadn't noticed.' Violet looked at Meredith ironically.

'But,' Meredith bit her lip, 'I didn't even know he knew.'

'He was only down at the stables when the panic started. By the way, Mr *Christian* had to leave—once I'd assured him you were all right, that is. He said he'd be in touch with you. He took Miss Healey home on his way. Now are you going to have that shower or do I have to make you?'

Meredith stared at her and found herself close to tears again—of frustration? she wondered.

But what Violet said next really floored her. She walked up and patted Meredith's shoulder and said kindly, 'I know. He's been giving you a hard time again, hasn't he?'

Meredith's lips parted. 'Who?'

'Why, Mr Evan, of course.'

'How . . .' Meredith broke off and closed her eyes.

'How do I know? I can see it in your face, and his, every time. Men!' Violet rolled her eyes heavenwards. 'And if ever I saw a right handful, he's it. Pity you had to fall for him, but that's what makes the world go round, so I'm told. Now *will* you go and shower before you catch cold, because that's the last thing you need!'

It was several hours later before Meredith could catch her breath, in a manner of speaking, because after dropping her bombshell, Violet had bullied her into the shower, commanded her back to bed, and then the doctor had arrived from Scone and he'd made an exhaustive examination before echoing Violet's sentiments on the state of her leg. Although he had added that a sudden, incautious movement could sometimes cause the muscles to go into spasm.

'I did,' she said involuntarily, 'do something like that last night. But I mean right here, in bed. It did hurt, though, for a while.'

'After you'd been lying quite still for a time?'

'Yes,' she said slowly, 'quite still.'

'Then that's probably it, Mrs Sommerville. Although,' he was the doctor who had given her regular check-ups once she had left hospital, so he knew her and her history, 'I do agree with Nurse Jenkins that you've been overdoing it, Mrs Sommerville. I think you've lost weight since I last saw you. I do think a couple of days of rest and only very gentle exercise might do you the world of good. And now,' he stood up, 'I think I'll go and see my other patient—who looked a lot sprightlier than you do, incidentally.'

Then Mrs Whittington brought her lunch and stayed to make sure she ate it, Mrs Sommerville came in for a relieved chat and Violet brought her a book to read.

'I've just finished it and I loved it,' she said enthusiastically.

'*Confessions of a Beachcomber*,' Meredith read, and looked surprised.

'E. J. Banfield wrote it years ago,' Violet told her knowledgeably, 'and it became quite a hit overseas.'

'Oh, *that* Banfield!' Mrs Sommerville said, as if she knew of at least half a dozen. 'The different drummer man. Why yes, I've read that too, Violet, and thoroughly enjoyed it.'

'It's your book,' said Violet. 'I found it in the study. Now what wouldn't I give to be on a tropical island with this nasty weather about!' she added, gazing out of the window at the teeming rain. 'He went there to die, you know, and ended up living another twenty-five years. Isn't that amazing?'

'Oh, *Dunk* Island,' Meredith said, suddenly enlightened.

'Mm. Of course it would be a bit changed now. There's a resort on it, but his grave is still there. I think I might go there for my next holiday,' Violet said dreamily. But she soon came back to reality and decided that Meredith should be left in peace to have an afternoon sleep. And once again she shooed everyone out and produced a little silver bell for Meredith to ring if she needed her.

Sleep, Meredith thought, when she had been left in splendid, almost royal isolation with her fire stoked up and burning brightly.

She looked around the Wedgwood blue and cream hangings and sighed. The rain was drumming heavily on the roof and gurgling in the downpipes, and she was really warm and comfortable, but her mind felt curiously stretched to the limits, taut, ready to snap—no, she thought restlessly, but for *Violet* to be able to discern what was going on ... Well, to have a fairly shrewd impression of some of the elements of the situation . . .

'Oh God, Meredith, don't skirt around the issue!' she said out aloud suddenly. 'Admit it!'

But the prospect that seemed to stretch endlessly before her mind's eye was terrifyingly bleak. To stay; no, that just wasn't possible. But where to go and what to do? She thought of her aunt in New Zealand who had come over after the accident, to visit her and offer her a home again when she was well enough. But she knew that although the offer was genuine, it wasn't practical, and even that, in her heart of hearts, her aunt thought she was better off with the Sommervilles. They still corresponded regularly, but not for a long time now had any mention been made of Meredith going to New Zealand except perhaps for a holiday.

She sighed and rather distractedly picked up *Confessions of a Beachcomber*, thinking that what she really needed was an electrifying mystery if anything.

Halfway through Chapter Two she fell asleep unknowingly and with a corner of her over-burdened mind refreshed and delighted. E. J. Banfield had had a way of painting a picture with words, a portrait of sparkling seas, tiny sunbirds, jungle, spider-lilies and cymbidiums and a paradise of 'scented silence' on his beloved Dunk Island. But the trauma of the previous night and her panic that morning finally took its toll.

She slept deeply and dreamlessly until dinner which she had on a tray, then started to read again with growing delight. Banfield had gone to Dunk with his wife Bertha, after being given only six months to live, to end his days on an uninhabited—by whites at least—tropical isle, in peace. Yet he'd lived for another twenty-five years on Coonanglebah, the Aboriginal name for Dunk.

Meredith read for hours, then she slept again, but to dream this time of the megapode, or bush fowl, and their mysterious mounds, of Brammo Bay and Purtaboi and a world that Evan Sommerville had no place in.

CHAPTER SIX

BUT Evan was the first person Meredith encountered the next morning.

The rain had gone, she saw from her bedroom window, leaving a cold but clear, sunny day in its wake with everything outside, plant, tree, paddock-fence, in sharp, clean ultra-focus. She could visualise her breath hanging on the air and Nuriootpa stamping the ground as she came out of a warm box and making her displeasure felt as they cantered along, then warming up and galloping for the sheer joy of it.

I can't stay here, Meredith thought, I feel too well. She grimaced ruefully. So she dressed warmly in ski-pants and an olive-green quilted jacket. Her leg, although a little stiff at first, responded beautifully to cautious usage and she was moved to thank God that her setbacks were only occasional because it could have been so much worse. Violet was right, however long it takes, it's worth it, she thought.

She also beamed up another thank you when it appeared, as she stole through the quiet house, that she was the first up.

But she had underestimated Evan. He was pouring himself a cup of coffee in the kitchen as she walked in with the same idea in mind.

She stopped dead and he looked up. Like her, he was dressed warmly in jeans and a thick mulberry sweater.

'I . . .' She swallowed and breathed uncertainly.

'Merry,' he said, transferring his gaze back to the

battered old enamel coffee-pot Mrs Whittington always left on the stove to be brewed up by whoever had an early start.

'I thought I was the first up,' she said quietly, and saw him raise an eyebrow.

'Should you be up at all?' he queried.

'I'm all right now. It wasn't anything serious. Evan,' she twisted her hands together, then took the plunge, unsure what was prompting her but conscious of the need to make a fresh start, perhaps consistent with this fresh new day, 'Evan, what you saw the night before last wasn't what you thought it was.'

He looked at her thoughtfully, then picked up his coffee-mug in both hands. 'You mean you and Chris,' he said flatly.

Meredith nodded and got herself a mug down from the dresser.

'What was it, then?'

The coffee was bubbling cheerfully in the pot and it steamed as she poured it out. She too felt like wrapping her hands around the mug in the early morning chill, but stopped herself for some illogical reason. 'Nothing really,' she said a little drily. 'He was being brotherly.'

Evan smiled and it was as cold as the air outside, she thought with an inward shiver. 'Well, why don't you ask him?' she said cuttingly, then bit her lip.

'I did,' Evan drawled. 'He ... er ... confirmed my opinion that it simply wasn't in his nature to be *brotherly* towards someone like you who wasn't a blood relation at all.'

Meredith stared at him with parted lips and stunned eyes. 'He didn't!' she exclaimed incredulously. 'He couldn't have.'

Evan shrugged. 'That was the distinct impression I

formed, my dear Meredith. So much so that when I spoke to the doctor I couldn't help wondering just what kind of sudden, incautious movement it was that so incapacitated your leg. Perhaps you're just not up to lovemaking yet, Merry,' he said gently.

'You *bastard*!' she whispered, and slammed her coffee-cup down on the table so that it spilled over.

'Perhaps,' he agreed dispassionately, 'but when it comes to brothers, or to be more accurate, brothers-in-law, might I remind you that I was first in line, Meredith, and that I've waited a long time.'

'F-for what?' she stammered, stuttering in her rage.

'Why, what our very first meeting promised and never delivered,' he said mildly.

'But that's crazy!' she flung at him. 'I saw you with Sarah last night—you *told* me you were thinking of marrying her—how can you? I don't understand! Yes, I do,' she panted. 'You're determined to get your revenge for what happened that night!'

'Is that so unthinkable? You've never explained.'

'You've never given me a *chance* to!'

'Well, here's your chance now,' he said through gritted teeth. 'Although I disagree that I've never given you . . .'

'Oh, but if by that you mean as I think you do, that I should get down on my knees and beg your forgiveness for leading you up the garden path—oh no! Never. Not you, Evan,' she all but shouted, and realised she was also shaking with an emotion so white-hot she wanted to do more than shout. She wanted to scream and throw things.

She ran past him instead out of the kitchen and slammed the door. And she stormed into her bedroom and slammed that door and sat down on her bed to bury her head in her hands, at the same time as the back kitchen door slammed at Evan's hands.

She was left to her rage and grief for about two minutes, then Mrs Sommerville came into her bedroom without knocking with Violet hot on her heels and Mrs Whittington not far behind.

Meredith lifted her head and groaned as she found herself confronted by three pairs of anxious eyes.

'Meredith, my dear,' Mrs Sommerville began, clutching her hastily donned dressing-gown about her. Violet was looking majestic in yellow candlewick and Mrs Whittington was dressed but still in her slippers. 'My dear Meredith,' Mrs Sommerville started again.

'I'm sorry. It's all right,' Meredith gulped, forestalling her. 'It was nothing really. I'm *sorry*.'

'Didn't sound like nothing to me,' said Violet. 'And anyway, what are you doing up?' she added in the tone of voice which suggested that if Meredith had stayed in bed, she might also have stayed out of trouble.

'No, it didn't,' Mrs Sommerville echoed, and even Mrs Whittington remarked that it certainly hadn't.

'I . . . I had a row with Evan,' Meredith said feebly, and got up abruptly.

'Not hard to do,' Violet murmured with an apologetic look at Mrs Sommerville.

'Oh, I agree entirely!'

'So do I.' Mrs Whittington nodded her head energetically.

Meredith closed her eyes and fought down an hysterical inclination to laugh, because she well knew that Mrs Whittington thought the sun shone out of Evan Sommerville, as did his grandmother, really. And even Violet bowed to his authority.

'Mrs Sommerville,' she said shakily, 'I . . .' She stopped and lifted her shoulders helplessly.

'Do you know what I think, Meredith?' Mrs Sommerville said. 'I think you need a holiday! After all, I interrupted your last one and ever since then you've been waiting on me hand and foot.'

'That's not quite true,' Meredith interrupted, but her objection was waved aside vigorously.

'More or less it is. Anyway, you're looking a little fraught lately. And—well,' Mrs Sommerville hesitated, 'you and Evan do seem to find it a bit of a strain being in each other's pockets.'

A bit of a strain! Meredith took a breath and found herself thinking suddenly of Ballina and that quiet room beside the river. 'Well,' she said uncertainly.

'Nor do I want you to think for one minute that you have to be tied to my apron strings, Meredith,' Mrs Sommerville continued. 'Of course Sommerville will always be your home, but never your prison. Perhaps the time has come for you to spread your wings, my dear,' she added gently.

Meredith stared into her grey eyes and could not speak. But she could think—here it is on a platter again, from Mrs Sommerville herself. I don't need to make any excuses, think up any reasons, feel quilty. 'I . . . perhaps you're right,' she said at last. 'I have thought for some time that . . .' She stopped awkwardly.

'And I've suspected it for some time,' Mrs Sommerville said. 'But I'm so fond of you, my dear, I've been a little selfish. Meredith, you do understand what I'm saying, don't you?' she added very anxiously then.

'I think so,' Meredith whispered.

'Then I can *trust* you not to disappear, to keep in touch with me and feel able to come back here to see me or stay in spite of Evan, this time?'

Meredith closed her eyes. 'You knew?'

'I wondered, and I can't tell you how sad it made me. But,' Mrs Sommerville shrugged, 'that's life.'

'Do you know why?'

'Ah, Meredith,' Mrs Sommerville said wisely, 'that's your own affair. No, but whatever, it never can make any difference to the way I feel about you. As if you were the daughter I never had.' She broke off as a door slammed and they all froze at the sound of Evan striding along the passage. But his footsteps stopped in the hall and after a moment or two of silence, they heard him speaking into the phone. As the gist of what he was saying, to Sarah Healey apparently, became plain, expressions of almost comical disbelief ranged across all their faces.

'Totally washed away, I tell you! The creek has broken its banks and every single new vine planted has disappeared. I always felt it was a dicey aspect.'

'Oh no!' Mrs Sommerville breathed, and they all flinched as the phone was slammed down.

Mrs Whittington was galvanised into action. 'I'll go and make his breakfast,' she said, and departed hastily.

'There are some days when life wasn't meant to be easy,' Violet pronounced.

'How right you are,' Mrs Sommerville agreed, and turned back to Meredith. 'Perhaps you were wiser than you knew when you decided not to come into this project with us,' she said whimsically. 'Now . . .'

'*Now*,' said Meredith. 'Right now, this morning. Do you mind? I just don't think . . .' She shrugged expressively.

'Well . . .' Mrs Sommerville looked doubtful.

But Violet seemed to think differently. 'Probably best, actually. He'll certainly have more than enough on his mind today. I'll help you pack.' She ran a practised eye over Meredith. 'Just promise me something. Take it *easy* for a few more days!'

'I will,' Meredith promised.

That night, Meredith fell asleep marvelling at how easy it had been to leave Sommerville. Well, relatively easy. Because at the last minute Mrs Sommerville had seemed a little conscience-stricken. 'I feel as if I've pushed you out,' she had said almost tearfully. 'I didn't mean it to be quite so precipitate. And I'm worried about you driving.'

'Please, I'll be fine,' Meredith had said, a bit tearful herself. 'And I understand, and it is for the best.' Then she had hugged the old lady and somehow that had said more than words could.

She'd been unable to avoid Evan, however. He had come out to watch her depart, his eyes still cold and angry, and he had said quite openly, 'Running away again, Meredith?' to everyone else's extreme embarrassment—bar Violet, who had smiled a not quite hidden little smile.

Meredith had tried to concentrate on what Violet could possibly have to be smiling about, and had kissed her three well-wishers once again. Then she had turned to Evan and held out her hand. 'Goodbye. I'm sorry I wasn't able to stick to the bargain.'

His grey eyes had held hers and he had ignored her hand. Then he had smiled, but not with his eyes, and taken her chin in his fingers and kissed her lips briefly. 'Goodbye, dear sister-in-law,' he had said, and even then, at that final point—surely he must know that's what it has to be between us, she had thought—his eyes had mocked her.

She had stumbled slightly down the steps and driven away in anger.

She had decided to spend the night in Newcastle and had called in to see Felicity early in the afternoon—to be greeted with some astonishing news . . .

'Merry! Merry! Guess what? Oh, I'm so glad you came!' Felicity had cried, flinging her thin little arms around Meredith's neck.

'You can walk on your own?' Meredith had hazarded.

'No! Yes, I can, and I'll be going home soon, but it's even better than that! Daddy's going to marry Sister. I thought I might get him to fall in love with you, but you always missed him.'

Some time later, Meredith had gone in search of the Sister she had first spoken to about Felicity.

'Yes, it's true,' she had confirmed, and smiled wryly. 'I believe you were Felicity's first choice, but,' she had shrugged, 'she seems quite pleased with me. It rather came upon me out of the blue. Ron, her father, always seemed so lost and lonely whenever he came down to see her and I sort of took him under my wing. Then . . .'

'I hope you'll be very, very happy,' Meredith had said softly, and been rewarded by a happy smile.

But later on, back in the motel where she had chosen to stay rather than the Sommerville residence, it had seemed as if it was her turn to be hit by a tide of loneliness. Which is crazy, she had thought. Felicity couldn't be in better hands, but . . . well, perhaps I enjoyed feeling a little responsible for *someone*?

She had stared sadly out the window and then shaken herself mentally and idly picked up *Confessions of a Beachcomber* which she had brought away with her to finish, only to be hit by a sudden brainwave. Why Ballina? she had thought, where I've already been and Evan's been too, for that matter. Why not Dunk? It was the start of a new life for E. J. Banfield. Maybe *I* could go there for a while and try to sort out a new life for myself, get some inspiration or try to go back to the beginning, to the person I once was?

She had riffled through the book with suddenly shaking hands for a passage that had stayed in her mind and found it finally. 'This was our very own life we were beginning to live; not life hampered by the wills, wishes and whims of others.'

She had lifted her head and let the book fall, and thought *yes.*

Which was how, after a flurry of activity, she had come to be in Sydney that night. She had arranged to garage her car and store some luggage—all of which she could have left with Chris, assuming he was in residence in Newcastle, but the same reluctance that had seen her choose to stay in the motel had held her in its grip. She couldn't honestly believe that Chris had lied outright to Evan, but she couldn't even begin to understand his motive in even lying by omission. Anyway, what difference does it make now? she had thought wearily, and taken a coach to Sydney, not even caring that she had had to pay for a night at the motel which she hadn't spent there. Because now she had made the decision, the urge to get to Dunk Island was overwhelming. And she was fortunate enough to be able to fulfil it the next day.

The flight to Townsville in North Queensland via Brisbane was uneventful and impersonal by jet.

The flight to Dunk from Townsville in a small Twin Otter aircraft of Air Queensland was pure magic. At an altitude of about a thousand feet, they floated over an aquamarine sea shaded with gold and pink in the late afternoon sunlight, from island to island—the Palm Group just north of Townsville, Orpheus, then the bulk of Hinchinbrook, the biggest by far, and finally, the Family Islands so named by Captain Cook, the pilot explained. Of which Dunk, the biggest, was the Father Isle and Bedarra the Mother Isle.

Meredith stared down, enchanted as the pilot named some of the smaller islands in the group, the children, and pointed out one of the family characteristics, a shelving sandspit on the north western corner of each island large or small like a white finger pointing into the sea. Then they circled Dunk and she recognised dainty Purtaboi Island off Brammo Bay from Banfield's description as they skirted the rocky, green-clad cliffs and spine of Mount Kootaloo, to make their landing-approach to Dunk over the bay.

Then they were down, a bare half-hour after leaving Townsville, and being greeted as they descended to the tarmac by smiling girls with flowers in their hair and bearing glasses of champagne and orange juice.

Meredith surrendered her ticket in the open-sided pavilion that was the airport on Dunk, and was welcomed warmly. 'Mrs Sommerville, let's see, you're in Captain Cook. You'll enjoy that, it's a beachside cabana and one of our nicest. In a minute or two I'll be driving everyone up, and don't worry about your luggage, we'll see to that.'

Friendliness, like the warm tropical air, was everywhere on Dunk, Meredith was to discover. And the girl who had welcomed her was right about the Captain Cook cabanda—actually a double cabin but with private verandahs and set, as was all the accommodation, amidst the most lush cool tropical greenery just above the beach that curved in an almost perfect semicircle around Brammo Bay.

There was a variety of accommodation, she had realised

during the short drive from the airport. A sweeping two-storied creepered block of rooms a little away from the beach, a much closer wooden block also two-storied, garden cabanas and then the beach cabanas on either side of the main resort buildings. On her side, the cabanas were very private and each named after someone to do with Dunk's history—Captain Cook who had discovered the island; Lord Montague Dunk, First Lord of the Admiralty at the time, whom Cook had named the island after, the Earl of Sandwich, another of his titles; Banfield . . .

But wherever you were situated, it was beneath a canopy of coconut palms or surrounded by flowering shrubs, trailing creepers and exotic vines and with wooden bridges crossing the natural waterways. Inside the Captain Cook, as Meredith was always to think of the cabana afterwards, the floor was tiled with cool, pale grey tiles, the walls and louvred cupboards painted white, the bedspread a royal blue with a deep pink hibiscus bloom nestled artistically in a fan of towels upon it, and the daybed also had a royal blue covering and cushions in hibiscus colours—pale orange, bright red, watermelon-pink. The two chairs and the occasional table were in white tubular plastic and there was a bowl of exotic fruit on the table. The bathroom was done in pale grey and white.

Meredith completed her tour of inspection, and stopped to stare at herself in the wide mirror of the built-in dressing-table, and with a sigh, felt herself relaxing.

She had three days of marvellous relaxation.

She lazed on the beach on a long lounger in a new swimsuit she had bought herself at the Blue Butterfly Boutique. She actually saw, on her first morning, the brilliant blue and black Ulysses butterfly that was the symbol of Dunk, skimming the air outside her cabana. She walked, mostly by herself, across the cricket pitch and the golf course to the farm, which provided fresh milk and cream for the resort; she walked around the north-west, sandy spit past the jetty and the deep-water end of Brammo Bay where all the boats anchored and one could hire catamarans or motor boats; she took a guided tour through the rain forest to Bruce Arthur's artist colony and admired one of his famous wool tapestries in the making, and tried to imagine herself living as they did in the middle of nowhere. It was the only other habitation on Dunk and perhaps, she thought, they see themselves as latter-day artistic Banfields. But at least he had lived close to the beach. She took a tour with Klaus, a resort guide, up Mount Kootaloo early one morning and actually saw the megapode and heard their weird, loud calls and saw one of their famous mounds where they incubated their eggs. And she went back several times to the quiet, dim clearing where Banfield's grave was and the ashes of his wife had been buried. The inscription on the stone grave was a quotation from Thoreau, but perhaps was, in this part of the world, now inextricably linked with Banfield, the first white settler to go to Dunk, to die—only to live a new life.

If a man does not keep pace with his companions perhaps it is because he hears a different drummer. Let him step to the music which he hears.

She also ate better than she had for ages, which was not hard to do in the huge dining-room with its half-walls, delicious meals and views through the palms to the sea. But apart from the people she shared a table with, mostly different at each meal, she kept to herself, although she was beginning to remember faces and receive friendly greetings wherever she went. Some, from seemingly unattached males, were more friendly than others, but she had no trouble dodging these.

Before she went to bed on her third night, she studied herself again in the mirror, and was pleased. No shadows under her eyes, a slight, pinkish sunburn subsiding into a deeper golden bloom and her hair not quite its usual glossy sweep but fuller and with curling tendrils and fairer—all the influence of sun and sea water.

But the real miracle, she thought, was how well she was sleeping, all night and half the afternoon.

At about midday the next day, she ordered herself a lemon squash from the waitress who patrolled the beach, and thought about going in to lunch. It was always a smörgasbörd of both hot and cold dishes and fabulous salads, sometimes so difficult to choose from, you ended up with a plate piled indecently high.

She had gone for an early group ride on one of the very docile steeds provided and under the expert eye of the riding instructor. Until, that was, he had lifted his eyebrows and grinned at her, and said, 'Don't need me, do you?' And he had wheeled away to concentrate on the novices.

It hadn't really been a ride, more a slow amble in the sunshine down the airstrip and then up into the rain forest. But the birds and the butterflies and the bush, and the view across Rockingham Bay to the mainland and Mission Beach, Bedarra, Hinchinbrook, purple and majestic in the distance and all the islands in between, had been superb.

'Tomorrow,' the riding instructor had said, ranging up beside Meredith on the way back, 'the tide will be right for a gallop along the beach. You should come.'

She had smiled fleetingly up at him and complimented him on how well-behaved his horses were, and how well he handled the novice riders.

'Never lost one yet!' he had said. 'Had a few want to get off before we'd even left the mounting-yard, with tears in their eyes too, but I wouldn't let 'em. And I've never had one who hasn't come back glowing with enthusiasm and pride.'

The comments in the visitors' book that all returning riders were asked to sign in the dairy, which was adjacent to the stables, bore this out. Meredith signed and wrote 'Wonderful', as she sipped her foaming, ice-cold vanilla milkshake—all returning riders got a fresh milkshake in the dairy.

But as she had wandered back to the resort across the golf course and the cricket pitch—named the Lord Montague Dunk Oval but affectionately known as 'Lords'—she hadn't been able to help thinking of Nuriootpa and who would be riding her now.

She had changed out of her jeans into her swimsuit, found herself a lounger, had a swim and then relaxed in the sun.

And now, she finished her lemon squash but found herself without the motivation to go to lunch, which lasted until two anyway. She lay back and watched the twelve-thirty Air Queensland flight from Townsville float in, and closed her eyes.

About half an hour later when she was not quite dozing and listening vaguely to the conversation of the two ultra-chic, ultra-sophisticated girls lying a few feet away from her, she heard one of them say, 'Well, well, look who's come amongst us. *A man!*'

Meredith felt a curious, feather-light trickle of apprehension run down her spine for no reason at all. But she moved restlessly all the same and heard the other girl say admiringly, 'Wow! Any chance of him being unattached, do you think?'

Meredith turned despite herself, and looked up—and went numb.

Directly in front of the lounge, another vast, high-ceilinged room that incorporated the bar and a dance-floor and had the same half-walls and roll-down canvas shutters as the dining-room, and was separated from it by an open deck, was the swimming-pool with its two Ulysses butterflies painted on the bottom. Colourful chairs and tables were set on the stone flagging around the pool and the flagging ended just a foot or so above the beach—that part of the beach Meredith had chosen that morning.

And there, indubitably, stood Evan Sommerville, with one hand shoved into the pocket of his long cream trousers and with his jacket suspended from his other hand over his shoulder.

And as she watched, almost terror-stricken, an errant wisp of breeze lifted his fair hair and fluttered the plain white cotton of his shirt briefly.

Where to go, where to hide. The frantic thought crossed her mind, but her limbs were locked, she found, in a way that had nothing to do with her leg.

She couldn't even look away. And inevitably, that scanning grey gaze found her.

By the time he had made his way down to her chair, she had moved, though. She was up, standing beside it defensively with, foolishly, her brightly coloured muslin beach-dress bunched up in her hands.

He said simply, 'Merry,' as he always did by way of greeting and let his gaze roam up and down her briefly but encompassingly—her bare golden legs, the green and white swimsuit, her bare shoulders and wayward hair.

She stared up at him and swallowed, thinking, how *can* you—how can you just say that? How can you do this to me? As if *nothing* has happened.

'What . . . what are you doing here?' she whispered out of a dry throat.

'I found,' he said levelly after a moment, 'that I had to follow a different drummer after all. You.'

Meredith dropped her dress but didn't notice. 'What do you mean? Why . . . how did you even know I was here?'

He smiled slightly. 'Last questions first. Violet dropped a great many hints, actually. I would have had to be a stone wall not to get her drift.'

'Violet? But . . .'

'She had this intuition. She said you were enjoying the book so much. It only took a few phone-calls to verify it.'

'Evan.' She stopped and realised to her horror that her eyes were clouding with tears and that the two girls a few feet away were sitting up and staring unabashedly.

Perhaps Evan understood one or the other of her causes of distress, or both, because he bent down then and retreived her dress, then said lightly, 'You chose a lovely spot, Merry. Incidentally, it's freezing back at Sommerville.' He grimaced. 'May I take you in to lunch? I passed by the dining-room on my way here and it's made me feel ravenous.' He handed her the dress.

She looked at it and then up at him and he said very quietly, 'Don't cry. I didn't come here to make you do that, believe me.'

She cleared her throat and found herself trying to smile for the benefit of the audience. 'All—all right,' she said huskily. 'I've been thinking about lunch for quite a while.

There's something about this place that does that to you—
makes you ravenous.' She slipped the shift over her head
and picked up her beach-bag. And, when he held out his
hand, she slipped hers into it helplessly.

How she got through lunch she wasn't sure, although she
did know that sharing a table helped. What hadn't helped
was staring down at her plate and discovering she had
much the same on it as she had had the night Evan, dressed
as a monk, had procured supper for her. She had looked up,
straight into his eyes, and known that the similarity had not
escaped him.

But he had poured her a glass of wine without asking her
if she wanted one, and she had been grateful because it had
seemed to give her a feeling of courage after a while.
Enough even to say, 'How are the vines? Did you manage
to rescue any?'

'No. We had to start again.'

'I'm sorry.'

'I suspect being a wine-grower was not meant to be a bed
of roses.'

But the general talk had been about other things. Have
you been to the reef yet? Isn't it fantastic? Well, to be
honest, the day we went it was so rough out there we were
all sick—think I might go by helicopter next time ...

Then there was no more excuse to be lingering, and
Evan stood up; Meredith got up too after the briefest
hesitation.

They walked out together and down the steps.

She said, 'Which way are you?'

'Same as you.'

'Oh.'

'Captain Cook.'

She stopped walking and stared up at him, but he took her hand again. 'Next door, actually. It was vacated this morning, I believe.'

'Did you,' her voice shook, 'did you ask for it? Did you even know that?'

'Yes. And yes. But you can lock me out, Merry, if you really want to. I won't have to sleep on the beach—just right next door.'

'Evan . . .' It was a bare thread of sound.

His grip on her hand tightened. 'Don't, Merry. Wait until we get there.'

'Oh God!'

They approached Captain Cook from the beach and just below the steps he said, 'Your place or mine? To talk.'

'Mine,' she whispered, and didn't really know why but thought she might feel safer in her room.

In fact, the sight of her possessions on the dressing-table, her cosmetics, her camera, a maroon-backed hairbrush with gold lettering on it, a small gold-mesh evening purse she used for dinner, and lying across the daybed, her jade-green terry-towelling robe, did give her a slight feeling of comfort, so that she turned around and said with something like decision, 'Evan, I . . .'

But she got no further, because he walked up to her across the cool grey tiles and took her into his arms.

She gasped and stiffened convulsively. 'No,' she said despairingly. 'You said to *talk*.'

'This might say more than any words can, Merry,' he murmured. 'But for the record, I've *missed* you and I'm sorry I forced you to leave like that. Kiss me.'

'No, no . . .' But the words died on her lips and her resistance, as always, she thought dimly, was astonishingly small to the feel of his mouth upon hers, his arms drawing her into the tall, long lines of his body, his hands on her back following the curve of it, one sliding up the column of her neck into her hair, the other on the swell of her hips, caressing and moving gently.

And to her utter despair, she didn't only kiss him back eventually, but she moved in his arms as if offering her soft slenderness to him, as if revelling in his strength and gentleness, as if . . .

She moaned, and Evan lifted his head at last and stared down into her slightly unfocused hazel eyes, at the soft colour in her cheeks, at her parted quivering lips. Then he picked her up and carried her to the bed.

She didn't protest when he laid her down on it, or when he lay down beside her. But that soft, lovely colour in her cheeks mounted hectically and she closed her eyes on the tears shimmering in them.

Evan ran his fingers through her hair and said her name, but she didn't stir.

'Look at me, Merry,' he said, his voice soft but commanding.

She did, at last, and shivered with pleasure as his fingers stroked her throat and slipped under her dress to the curve of her shoulder. He said, 'You asked me once how I could kiss the way I did. I have to ask you the same thing now. How can you kiss me back like that?'

Her eyes widened.

'And how can you feel the way you do in my arms?' he went on when she didn't, couldn't say anything. 'Willing, responsive, softening.'

He waited a moment, his grey eyes searching, she felt, right through to the depths of her soul. Her lips moved, but no sound came.

'I can answer them both,' he murmured, those wandering fingers slipping a gold strand of hair behind her ear and lingering there. 'We want ... we've *always* wanted each other. We—could talk about this until Doomsday, but that would never alter *this*. Don't you see?'

Her eyelashes sank down under the burden of truth his words had revealed. That truth she had so often sought to hide from herself. But ...

Her lashes flew up and the grey-green of her eyes darkened as her lips parted.

But he forestalled her with a twisted little smile. 'I know what you're going to say. Something about the things said and done between us, the people between us. But even they can't alter this.'

'They can, they *must*,' she whispered, and shivered again, but this time as if a chill finger had touched her heart.

He watched her for a moment in silence, then put his arms around her and pulled her head into his shoulder, to say into her hair, 'No. Not this basic emotion between us, Merry. Our reaction to it—yes. The outcome to it, perhaps. In fact, if you ever needed proof of that I can only offer you myself,' he said drily. 'Because I've often reacted very badly, but I don't suppose I need to tell you that. But,' he moved her away so that he could look into her eyes again, 'it's never gone away, has it? In all honesty and—for better, for worse, don't you think it's time we looked it squarely in the face and plumbed the depths of it?'

'What,' she murmured, then stopped. What if there are no depths, if this also burns itself out? she wanted to say but couldn't. What will I do if you find you still can't trust me after you've had me? What will I do then?

'What?' he queried.

Meredith bit her lip and buried her face in his shoulder again. She thought, what am I trying to say? That I love

you as I never loved Leigh? But how can I know that?
'Nothing,' she said against his shirt. 'Nothing.'

'Then—you agree?'

She trembled against him and thought of the futility of
saying no while she was lying in his arms the way she was.
'Yes.'

They lay like that, just resting together for a long time.
Then Evan started to kiss her again, slowly and lingeringly
until she began to respond to his wandering lips, her skin to
shiver beneath his fingers and her heart to beat slowly and
heavily at this infinitely gentle, timeless sort of acquaintance they were finally making.

He helped her out of her dress and she found herself
unbuttoning his shirt so that she could lay her lips and her
hands on his skin.

Then they were naked with nothing between them,
nothing to hide the fullness of her breasts pillowed on her
arm above the smallness of her waist as she lay on her side
facing him. He touched her nipples and traced the soft
round up-curve of first one breast and then the other,
saying huskily, 'I always knew they had to be exquisite.'

Meredith made a little sound in her throat and closed her
eyes, her own hands stilling on his chest.

But it seemed he didn't want that. 'Don't,' he murmured.

Her lashes fluttered up and he smiled slightly. 'That's
better. I want you to *share* this with me completely. I want
to be able to look into your eyes and know if I'm pleasing
you.'

'You are.'

'Then tell me, show me, reassure me. Shout if you want
to—but please don't lock anything in. You've been doing
that for too long.'

'Oh, Evan,' she said on a breath, 'perhaps I'm just made

that way,' she whispered.

'No!' he said almost fiercely. 'Look, I'll show you, but don't close your eyes, don't slip away.'

Is that what I do? she wondered dimly. But not much later, she was electrically alive with every nerve-end quivering and every intimate part of her body pulsing beneath his hands and lips, as she had never been before.

'Evan!' she gasped, wondering now how he could know her so well, her most sensitive spots, and know how to coax a response that made her feel hot and cold, made her break into a sweat but not care, made her skin tremble in some places before he even touched it as if it were separate from her mind and knew what was coming—that sweet torture that made her arch and curve against him and say his name in so many ways. Pleadingly, desperately, yes, no, I mean yes. No, I'm not slipping away—how could I? Oh God, Evan, *please*. I can't stand much more, I'm . . .

He held her head against his shoulder and her body hard against his as she lay in his arms, shuddering with pleasure and quite stunned. For this lovemaking had been for her alone and it had never happened to her before, not like that. If anything, it had quite often been the other way around with Leigh, with her concentrating solely on pleasing him.

It was a long time before Evan let her go, and then not completely but just enough so that they could look into each other's eyes.

It was a long, long look and she felt her cheeks beginning to burn as she remembered. Her lips parted, then she tried to turn her head away.

But he wouldn't let her. 'Say it,' he urged, his fingers beneath her chin, one of them caressing the outline of her mouth. 'Tell me if you liked that or hated it.'

'I . . .' But she found herself kissing his hand suddenly, warmly and spontaneously and with an uprush of emotion that brought tears to her eyes but also a shaky smile to her lips. 'I'll have to learn to shout louder,' she murmured. 'Thank you. Now it's your turn.'

Then she set out to repay him with delicacy and grace and expertise, using her hands and lips on his long, strong body, brushing her breasts against the hard wall of his chest and trailing the tip of her tongue on his skin. Only it wasn't long before she discovered how curiously hard it was to remain objective, how she didn't want to and how she had the strangest feeling that he didn't want her to.

She lifted her head suddenly and stared into his watching, narrowed eyes. 'It's normally never . . . any good for me twice. I mean . . .' She broke off with an odd little catch in her voice and discovered that she was breathing erratically again, and that she couldn't read his eyes at all.

Nor did he say anything, but he caught her wrists in one hand, and with the other, gently eased her over on to her back.

'Evan, I . . .'

'Shhh . . .' His breath fanned her cheek and he released her wrists and placed her arms by her sides and touched her breasts lingeringly.

'Evan,' she breathed, reaching for him suddenly, wanting him on top of her, within her, holding her.

He came into her arms and eased his weight on to her, and she closed her eyes and moved beneath him, glorying in the feel of his smooth broad shoulders beneath her hands. 'Evan, Evan . . .' she whispered, 'please.'

'Merry.' His lips trailed a devastating path down the column of her neck. 'Slowly, take it slowly.'

'How can I?'

'I'll show you.'

He did, with a sureness of touch that alternately took her breath away yet brought her back to the rhythm and pace he was setting so that that final intimate union of their bodies brought her no pain, only an infinite welcoming and joy. And when he saw this in her eyes, only then did he raise the tempo and tension gradually until they were moving as one and the glorious, shuddering moment of relief came to them both at the same time.

Oh, thank God, Meredith found herself thinking as she clung to him dazedly. Thank God it's happened for him too. I thought . . . But she couldn't quite formulate what she had thought and feared—yes, feared, she realised. His control?

But her fears and confusion were lost then, and she even wondered if her imagination had been working overtime, in the unbearably sweet, gentle aftermath of their lovemaking.

'All right?' he said eventually, still holding her and stroking the golden tangle of her hair.

'Yes. Oh, yes!'

'Come, then.'

Her lashes flew up, her eyes green with surprise, and he smiled and kissed the tip of her nose. 'Only under the sheet to sleep.'

Which she did a very short time later, still in his arms.

CHAPTER SEVEN

NEVER sleep with a stranger ...

The thought slid across Meredith's mind several times over the next few days like a line from a song or a bar of music that persisted in your brain. Where does that come from? she wondered. Evan could never be a stranger now. Was he ever? From that very first night ... how curious that was. But he did become a bitter, implacable enemy.

She cut off that set of thoughts with something like a shiver of apprehension. She couldn't help thinking of herself, though, and how she was oddly shy of him when they weren't in bed, although she tried to hide it. And how she occasionally felt like a young girl with her first lover instead of a twenty-two-year-old widow, a woman of the world now, surely?

But Dunk helped—how could it not? she marvelled.

They took up golf and played a couple of rounds every day on the scenic six-hole course, and although Meredith had never played before, under Evan's expert tutelage she managed even to be able to hit the ball, and anyway she loved the walking and the birdsong and the views. And the way Evan with no apparent effort whatsoever sent that little white ball soaring into the air, or putted with a delicacy of touch that should have surprised her but didn't—not now.

They hired a motorboat one day and took a picnic lunch and some fishing-gear over to Purtaboi, and by a stroke of luck had the island to themselves. Apart, that was, from the friendly honey-eaters, little yellow-and-khaki-striped birds with an enchanting song and a very bold front when it came to picnickers.

The next morning they hired a boat again but this time went in the opposite direction, round the north-west sandspit and then south to the little islet of Mung-um-gnackum where they picked oysters off the rocks, cracked them open and ate them just swished in salt water. They were the most delicious oysters Meredith had ever eaten.

In between these excursions and activities, Evan also taught her how to sail a catamaran, they ate and lazed on the beach and they danced after dinner to the resident band Papillon.

And they made love, sometimes in the evenings, sometimes in the mornings, sometimes the afternoon, sometimes when they should have been doing other things.

Like the night she was getting ready for dinner and Evan, who was already dressed, was lying on the bed watching her. From the very first, he had indicated that anything she did fascinated and intrigued him. He loved to watch her dressing and undressing, brushing her hair, even painting her nails. He liked to smooth on the body lotion she used himself, he liked to watch her waking up and going to sleep.

This night she had gone to iron a pale grey silky blouse and a grey cotton skirt with diagonal pink panels in it, and had to wait a few minutes for the use of the iron, which was how he came to be dressed and ready before she was.

'I won't be long,' she said, and automatically picked up her underclothes to go into the bathroom. But a sudden glance at him stopped her.

I suppose it's stupid to be shy, she thought, reading the look in his grey eyes.

It was just after she had put her bra on that he said, 'Do that again.'

'What?' She looked up.

'Put your bra on.'

'It is on. What's wrong?' She looked down with a frown.

'Nothing's wrong.'

'Then . . .'

'I just love the way you lean into it, that's all.'

'Oh.' She coloured faintly and turned away from the lazy grey glance he was sending her from beneath half-lowered lids.

'On the other hand,' he said, and she jumped because he had got up quickly and very quietly and was standing right behind her, 'you don't need one, do you, Merry? You're perfect without it.' She felt his hands on her back, undoing the clasp and then sliding the straps down her arms. He also reached around and removed the half-slip she had in her hands and put it and the bra on the bed. So that all she had on was a pair of lacy briefs.

They were standing facing the wide mirror above the dressing-table, and their eyes met in it, his still lazy and amused and hers wide and strangely wary.

'Why are you looking like that?' he murmured, and slid his hands around her waist.

'I don't know.'

'Do you mind me doing this?'

She watched in the mirror as his hands slid upwards to cup the milky white, round fullness of her breasts, and saw a pulse flutter at the base of her throat as his thumbs caressed the dark rose of her nipples and they started to swell and harden.

She closed her eyes on the image of herself standing virtually naked against him, her pupils a little unfocused with desire, that pulse beating and telling its own tale.

'Do you, Merry?'

'No . . .' It was barely a breath of sound and her eyes fluttered open, but Evan had bent his head and was kissing the soft hollow of her shoulders, and he didn't see what she saw, a sudden flash in her hazel eyes that seemed to say that she did mind but was powerless to do anything about it. But *why*? she wondered. I also love it. Who could deny that?

'Evan,' she whispered, but couldn't go on. Could only tilt her head back as a further invitation.

They were very late for dinner. In fact it was only the good humour of the staff that saw them not go hungry.

It was the next night, their fourth together, when things came to a head out of the blue. After her first dazed acceptance of what Evan had said the day he had arrived, Meredith had asked no questions and been in no condition to do anything but accept their mutual desire and its flowering.

But this night was a sparklingly chilly one. 'Got to remember it's mid-winter down south,' one of their dinner companions had said cheerfully. 'And this is nothing by comparison!'

No, it's nothing, she thought later, but all the same, she moved even closer to Evan on the dance-floor.

'Cold?' His lips moved on her cheek.

'Not any more,' she whispered.

Then the tempo changed, slowed, and Papillon slid into a very old number, *Blue moon, I saw you standing alone, Without a dream in my heart, without a love of my own.*

Meredith stiffened and, with a clarity that took her breath away, recalled another night and heard another band playing the same tune.

Her eyes widened and her mouth trembled as she stared up into Evan's grey eyes. Then with a swift movement, she pulled herself free and walked away.

He caught up with her on the square of lawn opposite the dining-room, but didn't say anything, and they walked in silence all the way to the Captain Cook. But when she hesitated on the verandah, he said, 'Oh no, Merry, it's too late to throw me out.'

She flinched, and he followed her inside and turned to slide the glass door shut and close the long curtains firmly.

'I gather,' he said, plugging the small kettle in and reaching for cups and coffee, 'that old tune resurrected some painful memories. Why don't you get changed, by the way? You'll be warmer in your robe.'

'I'm ... Evan ...' She broke off and bit her lip.

He waited for her to finish, standing watching her with a small bottle of brandy in his hands now, and that peculiarly arrogant tilt to his head, although his eyes were impassive, that had always frightened her.

'Well,' he said at last, 'you've wanted to talk about it, haven't you? Since I've been here, at least.'

She shivered in her flimsy dress, but from more than the unusual chill, and he put the bottle down and said impatiently, 'Damn it, Merry, you're *cold*. Have a hot shower,' he commanded. 'God knows, Violet already views me as something of an ogre when it comes to you, but if I take you back with a chill or your leg playing up—it isn't, is it?' he asked on a suddenly different note.

Meredith blinked. 'No! It's been marvellous up here. I think the warmth . . .' She trailed off. 'Did Violet say that?'

He grimaced. 'She didn't have to—one look of hers speaks a thousand words. And for what it's worth, I think she's decided to adopt us Sommervilles. I can see us *never* getting rid of her. But what are we talking about Violet for?'

'You brought her up.'

'Yes, because you're standing there looking pale all of a sudden, and shrivelled. Have a shower.'

Shrivelled, she thought dazedly, standing in a cloud of steam beneath a hot jet of water. What does he expect?

'Here,' Evan appeared in the bathroom with a pair of cream Viyella pyjamas in his hands. 'I found these. And don't stand there all night.'

She took a breath, feeling like a recalcitrant child, but he was gone and she could only stare at the closed door mutinously.

But a few minutes later, she appeared with her jade-green robe on over the long pyjamas. He glanced at her and boiled the kettle again, then poured the bubbling water on to the instant coffee. 'Black or white?'

'Black, thank you.'

'Sit down.' He brought her the cup and saucer and a packet of sugar and went back to pour the brandy, but she said quickly that she didn't want any.

'All right, let's talk, then,' he said. He didn't sit down but sipped his coffee leaning against the dressing-table, his eyes never leaving her face.

Her hands shook suddenly. 'I can't just *talk*,' she said huskily, with a shimmer of tears and anger in her eyes.

'Tell me about Leigh, then.'

'I ... what can I tell you?'

'You could start with Nadia von Brentlow.'

'You ...' Meredith stared at him incredulously with her cup halfway to her lips, '*knew*?'

'No. At least, not until after the party at Sommerville, a few days afterwards.'

'Who?'

'Sarah,' he said briefly.

'But I thought Sarah was overseas!'

'She was, at the time. Lavinia Marsh was not, however,' said Evan with a grim twist to his lips. 'I don't know if you know her, but we all grew up together.'

'I don't. Although I feel I should know her well. So—she told Sarah and Sarah told you?'

'Yes. She thought I ought to know what was being said about Leigh so that I could scotch the rumours.'

Meredith held his grey gaze for a long moment, her face perfectly expressionless, her eyes dark and shadowed. 'Have you?' she asked barely audibly at last.

He lifted his shoulders. 'I don't know how I could even if they weren't true. But they were true, weren't they, Merry?'

Her lips quivered and she looked away at last. 'Yes.'

'Why didn't you ever tell me?'

She bit her lip and looked down and her hair swung across her cheek.

'You don't like to speak ill of the dead?' he prompted on a curiously dry note.

'Something like that.'

'That's very noble of you, Merry.' His tone was openly ironic now and she flinched at it.

'What would you have done?' she said. 'In a similar situation?' She glanced up suddenly and caught his eyes narrowing.

'I think I would have made bloody sure,' he said softly but with an undertone of anger that also frightened her, 'that there were no possible misconceptions between us. Do you think I'd have been shocked to hear about Leigh? I doubt if I'd have even been surprised.' He looked at her a little contemptuously.

'You don't know that—you can't say that!' she cried. 'He was your brother in spite of everything, and you didn't know *me* from a bar of soap. Anyway, what difference would it have made? It didn't explain *everything*.' She fiddled distraughtly with her sash.

'It would have explained why you were feeling down,' Evan said quietly.

'Down?' She sniffed and licked her lips.

He shrugged. 'You know what I mean.'

'Down,' she repeated dully. Then a tremor shook her whole body. 'Confused, desperate, disbelieving, horrified, totally bewildered . . .' her voice shook, 'but none of that explains what happened. It makes it worse.'

'Does it? How?'

'You must know how. To fall into another man's arms just because your husband is being unfaithful to you.' She brushed away some tears with her knuckles, then stared up at him defiantly with her lashes sticking wetly together. 'What does that prove?'

He surveyed her dispassionately, then came to sit down opposite her. 'It might suggest,' he said quietly, 'that there was some very special magnetism between us. I felt it from the moment I saw you,' he grimaced slightly, 'standing alone beneath a blue moon.'

'Leigh,' her voice stuck in her throat, 'once told me the same thing—almost. And I thought I felt the same for him.'

'You were very young then, Merry. And alone. Has it occurred to you that he swept you off your feet?' His grey eyes were sombre.

She said honestly after a long hesitation, 'Yes. But,' she looked across at him in sudden tortured confusion, 'being very young shouldn't have altered my—I don't know what to call it—my morals? And anyway,' her voice sank, 'you make me feel very young.'

The look that passed between them caused her heartbeat to trip suddenly and a tinge of pink to come to her cheeks. She pressed her hands together awkwardly, 'I mean . . .'

'Compared to me you are,' he interrupted. 'You always will be younger,' he added with a suddenly wry look.

'But I'm not a girl any more,' she whispered.

'Is that how I make you feel?' he asked almost idly.

She stood up abruptly. 'You must know that, Evan,' she tried to say steadily.

'In bed?'

'*Yes*. And now, not only there.'

'Maybe Leigh wasn't a very good teacher, that's all.'

For a moment Meredith stood frozen as his words hung in the air. Then she said stiffly, 'I'm sorry about that. Perhaps I just wasn't a very good pupil. Then I suppose you've wasted these last few days.'

'I didn't say that at all.'

'Then *what*?' she flashed at him, her eyes suddenly furious and hurt.

Evan smiled slightly and for a moment she felt she could have killed him. But he said with a strange gentleness, 'You're very lovely in bed, Merry. I *meant* that I suspect my brother Leigh was more interested in his own pleasure than yours, that's all.'

'Surely it should be a mutual thing,' she managed to say drily.

'Oh, definitely,' he agreed. 'But until you realise and accept your own potential it . . .'

'Potential?' she broke in incredulously. 'What are we *talking* about?'

'Sensuality,' he said mildly. 'And accepting it,' he added

with a curiously significant glance.

'Evan,' she said shakily, 'this sounds so clinical, I can't—I don't think I want to hear any more. I don't want to think of it in those terms.'

'Neither do I.' He looked straight into her eyes. 'But if it's bothering you . . .'

'It's not that.' She bit her lip and wondered anguishedly what *was* bothering her. Because something about their lovemaking had been from the very first time, she knew. Nor was it that she hadn't enjoyed Leigh's attentions, but, she realised suddenly, what Evan had said was true. She had never ascended to the heights with Leigh that he could take her to, patiently, skilfully and until her body and mind were like quivering instruments over which he had complete mastery. But what was it that distressed her about it?

'Merry?'

She looked down at him to see him watching her carefully.

'Then if it's not that, we seem to be at cross-purposes,' he murmured at last.

'Yes,' she said dully, and sat down. 'As we always are,' she added.

'I was afraid that talking about it might not help,' he commented. 'Or are you trying to tell me that you don't think I'm any more trustworthy than Leigh was, Merry?'

'Perhaps,' she hesitated, 'it's myself I don't trust.'

'You were trying to tell me a minute ago how you're a woman now,' he said with an ironic look. 'But whichever, will you marry me?' he added with an abruptness that took her breath away.

She stared at him with parted lips and stunned eyes.

'Well, what did you think this was all leading up to?' he queried harshly.

'I . . . I . . .' she stammered helplessly.

'Do you want me to put all my cards on the table? Then I will. From the moment I first laid eyes on you I was—struck,' he said grimly. 'You were so young and beautiful and so innocent-looking, so tragic standing there in the moonlight. Yes, I saw it straight away and without even knowing you, I was moved in a way no woman had ever moved me before. And I knew I was going to have to have you—oh, it wasn't a conscious decision. It was more a kind of slow certainty. Which,' he smiled without humour, 'after a very short time, you seemed to confirm. I mean, it was as if the lightning had struck you too.

'Then I found out you were the one woman I couldn't have. But it was worse, I found out that my senses had played me false. That you were *apparently* a faithless, treacherous but oh-so-beautiful little bitch.'

Meredith flinched.

'I don't know what I was *supposed* to think, Merry.' His voice was harsh again and his eyes had narrowed at her movement of pain. 'Nor do I really understand why you persisted in hiding the truth from me for so long.'

'Because I didn't know the truth,' she whispered. 'I was ashamed, embarrassed, appalled, guilty. And a hundred times more so when Leigh died.' She took a breath.

'Even though you knew he'd fallen madly in love with another woman and was preparing to leave you—had married you on a whim apparently so that he could get you into bed?'

'I didn't know all those things at the time,' she cried. 'I thought I must have failed him, done something wrong,' her voice sank, 'not been alluring or exciting enough. I didn't know what to think. I even thought, who was *I* to point a finger after . . .' She stopped and looked across at him. 'How did you know all that?' she asked on a suddenly low, urgent note.

He shrugged. 'It was fairly common knowledge.'

'No. I mean—you used the very same words. You've spoken to Nadia, haven't you?' she accused.

He said evenly, 'Yes.'

'You shouldn't have done that, Evan.' Her voice was tight.

'In lieu of being able to speak to you about it, something I'd never been able to do successfully anyway, why not?' Evan countered drily.

'She really loved him, I think,' Meredith said with difficulty.

'Perhaps. They were definitely better suited, I should imagine. But that's beside the point. The point I'm interested in is why you never tried to explain at least. I know—I know I didn't make it easy in the beginning. But lately,' he paused briefly and a nerve beat in his jaw, 'you could have tried. It was only what I wanted to hear.'

Meredith dropped her head into her hands, shaken by so many emotions she couldn't think straight. But gradually several thoughts emerged from the chaos—that there was still something about her that angered Evan Sommerville deep down. She had seen the expression of it so often, seen him do battle with it, seen or rather *thought* mistakenly over the past few days that it, at least, had gone. Or if not that, that he had come to terms with it. But she was too familiar with it not to recognise now that it was still there and that nothing she could say would send it away. Why? Because in his heart he knows he won't ever be able to trust me?

Because—a sudden flash of intuition gripped her—he can never forget that I belonged to Leigh first. Are those the reasons for his almost awesome control when he makes love to me?

And finally she thought, all I want to hear is that he loves me, not wants me and needs to have me but *loves* me. Me, as I am now, not that false image of me in a medieval costume beneath a blue moon, so young and innocent, undefiled by his brother Leigh of all people.

'I can't,' she whispered.

'What?'

'Marry you.'

'Merry!' His voice cut the air like a knife and she shivered and made a frightened little gesture with her hands.

'No, Evan, please . . .'

'Then tell me why not.'

'I don't know if I can put it into words,' she faltered, tearing her gaze away from his pale, grim face and glittering grey eyes.

'You haven't enjoyed these last few days, then?' he said sardonically.

'It's not that,' she whispered. 'You must know that I have. I just don't think that we have the right ingredients for a,' her voice shook, 'marriage. Sarah Healey is probably a better bet for you . . .' She trailed off and her eyes widened in horror because that sentiment had escaped her involuntarily, as if some subconscious part of her mind had thrown it up like a splinter that had been festering there.

'You don't have to be jealous of Sarah,' he said tautly.

'I'm not.' Am I? she wondered with a sudden pang of fear, and realised with dismay that if she wasn't jealous, she *was* angry about Sarah Healey. After all, why should all the explaining have to be on her side? 'You did say once . . .' Some of that anger seeped into her words. 'How many women do you want to marry, Evan?'

'I never had any intention of marrying her, Merry.'

'But you said it had crossed your mind.'

He stared at her for a moment with his lips set in a hard line. Then he said, 'Yes, it did. Mainly because she was there for the taking, virtually, and it dawned on me how uncomplicated it would be, but . . .'

More than a seepage—something more like a gust of anger now shook Meredith. 'Then you used her, Evan, if that's true. But you know what I used to wonder? I used to think that if I ever gave in to you, that would be your revenge for what had happened and that it would be my punishment to have to see you *still* marry Sarah Healey.'

He went white under his tan and for one horrible, tense moment she was afraid of what he would do to her. But in the end, he only stood up and said dispassionately, 'If that's what you really thought, I can see why you don't want to marry me. Although it's a contradiction too, isn't it, Merry?'

'What do you mean?' she whispered.

'You work it out. And you were right, I did use Sarah.' He stood with his head bowed for a moment. 'For which I apologise—to you both,' he said barely audibly.

'Evan.'

'No, Merry,' he said very quietly, 'you've been right all along. There's too much between us. I'm only sorry I didn't understand sooner. Will you be all right?'

She said hoarsely, 'Yes, but . . .'

'Don't be afraid to come back to Sommerville,' he interrupted, and took the hand she had raised in something like despair. 'I doubt if I'll be there much from now on, but anyway, even if I am, it's *over* now. You,' he stared down into her hazel eyes and slid his fingers down to encircle her slender wrist, 'you should try to put both Leigh and me behind you and start again. If,' he went on with an effort, 'anything I've said tonight has given you the impression that you're anything less than warm and tender and wonderful in bed, I'm sorry for that too. It wasn't what I meant.'

'Evan,' she breathed, but he raised her hand to his lips and kissed it gently. 'Be happy, Merry,' he murmured, and returned her hand to her lap. Then he glanced around briefly, but there was nothing of his in her room, and he walked out, sliding the door closed behind him.

Meredith stared down at her lap, but a haze of tears blurred her vision. She waited in a frozen sort of vacuum, but she didn't hear his door open and knew he must have gone somewhere else—for a walk or back to the bar perhaps.

Finally she lay down, but she was still waiting to hear his door or some sounds from the room next door, without knowing what she would do when she did—knowing only that what she had achieved tonight seemed to hurt her more than anything else that had ever happened to her.

She fell asleep finally in a turmoil of misery and exhaustion.

She woke the next morning with her heart pounding and her mouth dry. She dressed with shaking hands, but she knew as she stepped out on to the verandah what she would find next door.

Evan was gone, and there was a resort maid just about to enter the room. 'Morning!' she called cheerfully to Meredith. 'You might be getting new neighbours today.

Mr Sommerville was called away urgently, apparently. He even chartered a flight to come and pick him up. Must say I'm sorry to see him go—his room was the easiest to keep clean on the whole place! I sometimes wondered if he ever used it except for his clothes and things.'

Meredith turned away precipitately and fled.

The clearing around Banfield's grave was dim and quiet, although from across the swinging bridge Meredith could hear the megapode calling and she thought of Banfield's description of their crow, 'a discordant and uncouth effort to imitate a rooster, as if it had been practising "cock-a-doodle-doo" all its life and had not yet arrived within quavers of it.' Soon they would fall silent, she knew as day succeeded the early dawn hours. Evan must have left very early.

A silent tide of weeping rose up within her and she put her hands to her mouth to stem it. But what else could I have done? she asked herself torturedly.

Presently, when she felt calmer but only because she was totally drained, she moved round to study the inscription on the grave again. But instead, her eyes fell to the one below it. Bertha Banfield had been devoted to her husband, had been alone on the island with him for three days after his death until a passing steamer had come to the rescue, had said once, 'You know that my life was for him, and beyond that there is nothing to be said.' Which her inscription on the stone grave bore testimony to:

Whither thou goest will I go, and where thou lodgest I will lodge—where thou diest, I will die, and there will I be buried.

Was she ever torn by doubts? Meredith wondered. Should it be enough for me to know that I *love* Evan, I can't help it, whatever his feelings for me might be. I can't doubt that now because I feel as if a part of me has been wrenched away, I feel as if I'll be lonely for the rest of my life and in despair. Yet I let him go. I thought—what did I think?

She raised her eyes to follow a mote of sunlight falling through the leafy canopy, a slim shaft of golden light with particles floating lazily through it, only to disappear.

I thought, I've suffered enough at the hands of two men, brothers. I've been the possession of one to be discarded at whim—she winced and closed her eyes—and I've come into the possession of the other who can't forgive me, so how can he love me? Who hates to love me—Chris got it the wrong way round. Oh, Merry, he's right, it's time to put it all behind you now, to start again somehow, it's the only way.

'But if *only*,' she whispered aloud, 'I could have found a way to tell him that something did strike me that first night, even though I couldn't understand it or accept it at the time. It must have, or I would have been able to tear myself away years ago, *somehow*. But I just couldn't break free, and even now when I have, I think I've broken my heart in the process. Why couldn't I tell him that and make him understand and believe it?'

Because you've never really admitted it to yourself, until now, Meredith, perhaps? she answered herself. Because you've kept telling yourself for so long that you didn't have the right to love another man so it couldn't have happened? Only it did, and a part of you has been ashamed and guilty ever since. Have you been harder on yourself than anyone else would have been?

'I don't know, I just don't know,' she murmured, and

brushed away her tears. 'Anyway, it doesn't solve the problem—there's something that stops me and Evan communicating fully, even now. And for all time?' She buried her head in her hands and wept, because the answer was obviously yes.

CHAPTER EIGHT

'COFFEE, tea or me, did I say that?' Laura Watkins asked Meredith, her brown eyes sparkling with merriment in her bright young face.

'You did,' Meredith confirmed. 'Thinking of becoming an air hostess?'

'Ah! No, but of course that's where that famous saying originated, didn't it? No, not at all! I'm perfectly happy working for you, darling Merry, in the chicest coffee-shop in Townsville—you do realise Chez Merry has become the *in* place, don't you?'

'Well, one of them,' Meredith conceded, and had to smile. 'But what brought the coffee, tea or me bit up? Just our general surroundings?' She glanced around with pride and affection. Chez Merry was not very big, but it was chic. Yellow-and-white-checked tablecloths bedecked the dark pine tables, the walls were panelled in the same pine as was the discreet counter, the carpet was yellow, filmy-white ruched curtains hung in the bow shop-front window which she had had remodelled and lush green pot-plants flourished in lovely old gleaming brass and copper kettles and pots. Added to this, as soon as one entered the dim and cool interior of Chez Merry—it was air-conditioned against the fierce tropical heat of Townsville—the lovely aroma of freshly ground coffee assailed the senses. Not that coffee was all they sold, although they did a roaring trade in iced coffee as well, in the middle of the day, but they also specialised in fresh-fruit punches and exotic ice-cream sundaes as well as light snacks and traditional gateaux like Laura's Black Forest cake.

And in only six months, Meredith mused, we've started to make a rather nice profit. 'Sorry,' she said hastily as she realised Laura was speaking. 'What was that?'

'I was saying,' Laura pouted whimsically, 'that *you* brought up the coffee, tea or me bit.'

'*I* did?'

'In a way. That last man you served—the rather nice-looking one in a sort of scholarly way—well, he looked at you as if he'd rather have you than his coffee. Didn't you notice? Oh, he's gone now,' she said as Meredith looked around ruefully.

'No, I didn't.'

'Did you notice him at all?' Laura demanded.

'Er . . . not particularly,' Meredith said apologetically.

Laura Watkins sighed a little exasperatedly and shook her brown curls at Meredith. 'I don't understand you, Merry. To have *all* the guns and never to use them, it's just not right! Don't you like men?' she asked. 'Personally I do!'

'It's not that,' Meredith murmured with a grin, thinking reminiscently of the succession of beaux Laura had had in the last six months. 'When the right one comes along . . .' She waved a hand expressively.

'What I'd like to know,' said Laura, 'is how you're going to know who is the right one. You never give them a chance to get to first base. *I* think . . .'

But what Laura thought was not destined to be uttered, not then anyway, rather to Meredith's relief, as a gaggle of customers came in signifying the start of the busy lunchtime session.

And fortunately, by the time Laura was due to go off — they worked a system of shifts, one of them on from ten until two, then six to midnight, while the other worked the full day from nine to six and they switched around weekly—by the time Laura was due to go off at two, she seemed to have forgotten about it.

So had Meredith, as she let herself into her unit on Melton Hill. But an inspection of her mail revealed a letter from Mrs Sommerville, her precise copperplate handwriting on the envelope was unmistakable, and Meredith stared at it and sighed, and found herself strangely loath to open it. Because of course Sommerville would always be linked with what Laura had been saying, but not only that. It was getting harder and harder to put off going to see Mrs Sommerville—it had been over six months since she had seen her, since she had left Sommerville in anger and gone to Dunk.

She left the letter unopened on the dining-table and made herself a cup of tea which she took on to the verandah, then she sank down into a cane chair and stared at the view as she drank it.

Townsville was dominated by Castle Hill with its sheer, bald summit of pinkish rock, its twin flanks of Stanton Hill and Yarrawonga and almost right above the foreshore towards the docks, Melton Hill. The view from Meredith's rented unit on Melton Hill was superb. Magnetic Island lay only a few miles off-shore and Cleveland Bay curved out to sea and Cape Cleveland. Meredith had watched the view in all different lights, seen the sea in the early morning when it was the palest blue and had the texture of stretched silk, seen the new casino on Breakwater Island inch up gradually, and she had never failed to be enchanted by it.

And now, well into summer, Melton Hill was ablaze with bougainvillaea and frangipani.

It had been a spur-of-the-moment decision to stay in

Townsville once she had left Dunk Island two days after Evan had left, made because the thought of going to Sydney or Newcastle had quite honestly frightened the life out of her, and because the winter warmth of the tropics seemed to agree with her leg, made because Townsville was one of Queensland's bigger cities and as such might offer her something to do.

Although what, had proved a real dilemma for the first couple of weeks. To go back into a bank, always assuming she could get back into one, didn't appeal to her, but that was all she was trained for. So she had searched the papers for a job, any kind of a job to take her mind off herself, but curiously, it had been a bank which had come to the rescue. At least, the manager of the bank she patronised, whom she had gone to see to arrange her affairs and transfer her account to Townsville. They had chatted for a while and Meredith had mentioned that she was looking for something to do, not terribly successfully so far, and the manager had grown thoughtful and then wondered out aloud whether she had thought of investing in a business.

She had not, and at first the idea had terrified her because she felt she was totally un-business-orientated. All the same, she had gone through the businesses for sale column of the paper and noticed the coffee-shop. She had taken the paper into the bank the next day and the manager had offered to look into it for her. His news, a few days later, had been encouraging. The present owners had been under-capitalised and anyway had run into family problems. But the position of the shop, just off the busy Flinders Street Mall, had definite potential, he had felt, and it was going for the proverbial song. What it needed, he had added, was someone with some capital and flair.

Meredith had spent a few agonising days wondering if

she had any flair, then she had thought of the state of her life and decided to take the plunge.

That she had succeeded far beyond her expectations and in such a short time still surprised her, although she always insisted on giving Laura a fair share of the credit. For the fact was that Laura was not only businesslike and energetic, but she had also been born and grown up in Townsville and seemed to know half the population *and* was a superb cake and pastry cook. She had actually answered Meredith's advertisement for staff in her own inimitable manner. She had arrived for the interview laden down with cakes and pastries of her own making. But more than that, they were roughly the same age and they had clicked as friends. In fact Meredith had lately been thinking of offering Laura a partnership.

All in all, she reflected, as she sipped her tea, it had been a very busy and productive six months and there had been times when she really thought she had shaken off the shadow of Evan Sommerville. Or if not that, at least nearly managed to seal off that part of her herself that missed him almost unbearably, that part of herself that sometimes ached for the slow rapture of his lovemaking, that part of herself that was afraid she had made an awful mistake.

But she had kept in touch with Mrs Sommerville as she had promised and often received enthusiastic letters in return, congratulating her on the success of the coffee-shop, telling her of Chris's latest exploits, and Violet's, telling her how the winery was going and so on. But she never mentioned Evan.

Chris had written to her once, though, and had mentioned Evan—it would have been hard not to, because he had written to apologise for what he had termed his 'irresponsible behaviour' after the party. 'When Evan accosted me the following morning, Merry,' he'd written, 'I'm afraid to say I refused to explain that little scene he walked in upon in the kitchen. I even went one further—I hinted that I'd had my eye on you for quite some time. Please believe me, it was a spur-of-the-moment lapse for which Evan himself was partly the cause—you know how high and mighty he can be sometimes, as well as critical and puritanical as if he himself would never . . . but be that as it may. My other impulse was, I realised later, a probably quite irrational attempt to make him jealous and *do* something about it—such as finally claiming you for his own. I don't think I ever told you that from way, way back I suspected Evan might want you for himself, did I? Anyway, I thought I had to let you know that I've felt terrible about it ever since. I've also confessed to Evan and actually, he was very nice about it. He said he hadn't really believed it anyway—which dented my ego slightly as it shouldn't—but that he'd been in a foul mood . . .'

Chris had gone on to say that it was obvious things hadn't worked out the way he had hoped for her and Evan, much to his sorrow.

And she had written him a light-hearted note in return, absolving him, although her heart hadn't been light at the time.

But if Chris's letter had cleared up a small mystery, it had solved nothing. And then there were Mrs Sommerville's letters that always ended with a heartfelt plea for Meredith to take some time off to go down and see her.

And each time Meredith had searched her heart and decided that that sealed-off part of her was a rather flimsy affair at best, and that to put it to the test by actually confronting it with Evan might not be wise. After all, sometimes just the glitter of moonlight on dark waters was enough to remind her of Dunk, and of him.

She sighed and realised she was sitting in the dark, so she went inside and made herself read the letter. It was quite short.

'My dear Meredith,' she read. 'Oddly, or perhaps not so oddly, I find myself missing you very much at the moment. I mean *more* than normal, and do you know why? Well, I think it's because my birthday is approaching and by the time you get to eighty-two, I suppose you can't help wondering if you'll see the next one. Now don't for one minute think that I'm feeling sorry for myself or that I'm sick—I'm not! I always did like to make a fuss about birthdays and if you were to come down it would make it just marvellous. Actually, I have to confess that I am feeling just a little sorry for myself—Evan will be away overseas and Chris is so busy being a business magnate these days, almost reformed, I would say (can you picture it!!!), I don't suppose he'll be able to pop by for more than a few hours. So it will be me and Violet and Mrs Whittington! What a prospect, fond as I am of them!

'Do you think you could rescue me from it?

'Love as ever,
'Amelia Sommerville.'

Meredith bit her lip and re-read the letter. Then she looked at the calendar in the kitchen. It was a week away and plenty of time to make arrangements to take some time off, although . . . But what if she *is* unwell, or simply failing a little? At eighty-two it wouldn't be unnatural, would it? *Would* I ever be able to forgive myself if something happened to her? And Evan won't be there . . . she must know that something has happened between us because she's never mentioned him before and that sounds like a subtle hint . . .

Five days later she was on a jet to Sydney.

Six days later, she braked her rented car on the gravel below the verandah of Sommerville and climbed out a little stiffly. She had driven up from Sydney and no one knew she was coming. She had decided to surprise Mrs Sommerville.

It was Violet who appeared first on the verandah, took one look at Meredith, then raced inside again calling jubilantly. It was Mrs Whittington who appeared next, and then Violet reappeared with Mrs Sommerville on her arm and Meredith was up the stairs and they were all kissing each other and laughing and crying happily.

'You came, you came!' Mrs Sommerville smiled, patting Meredith's cheek. 'Oh, my dear, I'm so thrilled to see you. And you're looking wonderful! Oh, this will be one of my very best birthdays!'

It was Evan who appeared last on the verandah.

And as they each became aware of him standing just outside the doorway, they fell awkwardly silent in turn, perhaps because Meredith had tensed so visibly, and paled a little.

'Merry,' he said into that pool of silence, his grey eyes capturing hers, 'this is a surprise.'

'Hello, Evan,' she heard herself saying as if from far away, and she wondered if anyone else could hear her foolish heart beating like a drum. 'I thought you were overseas.' She swallowed and cursed herself inwardly because that was as good as saying—if I'd known you'd be here I wouldn't have come.

'Oh, he was!' Mrs Sommerville launched herself into speech. 'Until only yesterday—at least, he only got home yesterday. Didn't you, Evan?' she appealed to him.

He smiled slightly at his grandmother as if to reassure her

and said with an undercurrent of wryness, 'Yes, I did. I'm afraid I had a change of plans rather unexpectedly. But Gran is right, you are looking well, Meredith. Come in—I'll get your bags. In the boot?' He looked at her with an eyebrow raised and she nodded and handed him the keys. Their fingers brushed, but he only turned to Mrs Whittington and said, 'I think this calls for a celebration, don't you? If you break out some of your very best fruit cake, I'll break out the sherry.'

'Oh yes, Mr Evan!' Mrs Whittington said fervently. 'I'll do just that!'

Meredith looked round the Wedgwood-blue and cream bedroom that night as she got ready for dinner and for a moment it was possible to imagine that she had never left it. There were still clothes of hers hanging in the wardrobe, clothes she had left behind, and some cosmetics set out on the dressing-table that she had left behind too.

She stared at herself in the mirror and forced herself to think about Evan and the fact of his being at Sommerville. She couldn't believe that Mrs Sommerville would have intentionally deceived her. No, she mused, but Mrs Sommerville—for that matter, Violet and Mrs Whittington too—obviously know that whatever was between me and Evan has ended in the negative, which is why they've been thrown into such a flutter, poor darlings.

And she had to smile at her reflection as she recalled three varying denials of any knowledge that Evan would be at Sommerville to coincide with a visit by Meredith.

Mrs Sommerville had been first off the mark.

'Meredith, my dear,' she had said extremely anxiously at the first opportunity, 'I didn't expect Evan to be here. You see ...'

'It's all right,' Meredith had broken in. 'Really. I would have come anyway.' She had taken Mrs Sommerville's veined hands with their swollen knuckles into hers. 'I just couldn't miss your birthday. You know, if I look half as good as you at eighty-two, I'll be happy. I've missed you too.'

'Oh, Meredith!'

Mrs Whittington had been next to waylay her. 'Mrs Meredith,' she had said awkwardly and twisting her pristine white apron in her hands, 'we didn't really expect ... we thought Mr Christian might come up, but we didn't ...' She stopped and looked supremely unhappy.

'It's all right, Mrs Whittington,' Meredith had said gently. 'It really doesn't matter. She's looking well, isn't she? Mrs Sommerville.'

'She's bearing up,' Mrs Whittington had replied, and added indistinctly, 'If you're sure?'

'Quite sure. Nothing could make me sorry I came. I've missed you too, you know.'

'Oh, thank you.'

Violet had been much more direct.

'He's not supposed to be here, you know,' she had said after entering Meredith's bedroom with the barest token knock and with a most unusually militant expression on her broad, plain face. 'He's—how's the leg?'

'Fine, Violet. It's been fine, honestly.'

'Good. He ...'

'Violet, it's all right.'

'He wasn't supposed to be home for another week. He turned up *right* out of the blue yesterday and of course we didn't know whether you *were* going to come.'

'That's my fault,' Meredith had murmured. 'But there's absolutely nothing to worry about, Violet.'

Violet had snorted and said, 'Then there should be.' But she had refused to elaborate.

All of which, Meredith mused, as she got up and reached for her dress, involved me in the telling of some lies. How is it going to be all right, for example? And *would* I have come anyway? Not that I can regret coming for Mrs Sommerville's sake.

She dressed absentmindedly in a coral-pink linen straight sleeveless dress and matching pumps. Then she fixed a chunky turquoise and silver brooch to the dress. Her golden tan had darkened slightly since she had taken up swimming in the Tobruk Pool on the Strand below her unit. And Mrs Sommerville had commanded that they have a celebration dinner tonight although it wasn't quite her birthday yet.

Oh God, I wish Chris were here, Meredith thought as she prepared to leave her room.

Yet, several hours later, she had to admit that dinner hadn't been the ordeal she had feared. Evan had gone out of his way to be charming and talkative, Mrs Sommerville had been bubbling with happiness and Violet who had joined them had been quite funny on the subject of some of her patients. Even Evan had grinned and remarked that she should write a book.

'I just hope I don't feature in it,' Mrs Sommerville had said wryly.

'Mrs Sommerville, I can honestly say you've been the best. It's been a real pleasure,' Violet had replied, and to their surprise, blinked away a tear.

Mrs Sommerville had said hastily, 'But you're not thinking of leaving me, are you, Violet?'

'Not so long as you need me or can put up with me,

ma'am.'

'Oh, Violet!'

Evan's grey gaze had caught Meredith's and his left eyelid had flickered in just the slightest suggestion of a wink.

But after Mrs Sommerville had gone to bed, Meredith had wandered out on to the verandah and thought with a sudden pang that she hadn't been down to see Nurioopta or even enquired after her. But it was too late now and ... well, there was *nothing* she could do now to stop herself thinking about Evan.

So civilised, she marvelled, as she leant lightly against a stone pillar. He meant what he said when he said it was over now. Perhaps he only ever needed to get me out of his system by sleeping with me.

She turned at a movement behind her and Evan moved out of the shadows and the verandah light glinted on his fair hair and cast a long dark shadow behind him.

'Merry,' he said. 'Would you like a nightcap?'

'No ... On second thoughts, I would.' She smiled up at him. 'It's—it's lovely out here, isn't it? Townsville is *very* hot at the moment.'

'Stay there, then, I'll bring them out.'

He came back a few minutes later and handed her a glass. 'But you like it, despite the heat?' he said.

'Yes.'

'Tell me about the coffee-shop.'

She did as they sipped their drinks side by side, quite fully, even going into figures.

He looked down at her eventually, rather quizzically. 'I had no idea you were so ...'

'I'm not really,' she broke in. 'Without my bank manager I'd be lost, probably.'

'All the same, you've done extremely well by the sound of it. Thought of expanding at all?'

'Well,' she hesitated, 'I had thought of opening a boutique. But one with a difference—Townsville is so hot, but if you're anything over a size twelve, it's hard to get reasonable, well designed,' she shrugged, 'tropical gear. You know, cool, summery clothes that don't make you look bigger anyway or expose you unkindly.'

'What does your bank manager think?'

She smiled faintly. 'His wife is an ample size sixteen.'

'Is there a way to clothe an ample size sixteen coolly but not unkindly?'

'It helps if you don't use violent florals.'

'Merry,' he said with a slow smile at the back of his eyes, 'I can see we've been unsuspectingly nurturing a genius in our midst. I have a feeling you'll go from strength to strength.'

She turned her head away. 'And you?' she asked after a moment. 'Is it going well for you?'

He said nothing, and she turned back to see him staring at his drink.

'Evan?' she said uncertainly.

He looked up at last. 'Very well.'

'You're not—you're not concentrating on the winery or Sommerville so much now? At least I gather not.'

'No.'

'And Chris is . . .'

'Doing surprisingly well?' he supplied. 'Yes, he is. I'm concentrating on new projects and he's running the rest of it.'

'What about the winery?' she asked.

'It's coming along surely but slowly. Sarah has left and gone back overseas, but in her place we have an earnest young man from Nuriootpa, of all places, in South Australia, so he has a very wine-orientated background and a very discerning palate.'

'Oh.' Meredith looked a little blindly, straight ahead into the darkness.

'Have you made many friends, Merry?' he asked presently.

'One.' She told him about Laura.

'No ... men friends?'

'No.'

'It will come,' he said. 'For you it has to come.'

'And ... and for you?'

'No, no one special. By the way, talking of Nuriootpa, the horse, I was wondering if she shouldn't be put in foal ...' He stopped as a French window further down the verandah flew open unexpectedly and Violet staggered on to the verandah through it, just as if she'd been leaning her weight against it with it not properly closed, in a classically eavesdropping pose.

But she righted herself and even managed to say nonchalantly to them, 'Beautiful evening, isn't it? Thought I'd just take a little air.'

'Oh, beautiful,' Evan agreed sardonically. 'Do join us, Violet.'

Violet looked fleetingly confused and guilty, but she said, 'No, no! Think I'll go for a little walk. Don't let me ... er ... disturb you.' And she set off down the steps, tripped once but kept going although her broad back radiated embarrassment and a forlorn attempt at dignity.

Meredith leant back against the pillar again and found herself shaking with silent laughter.

But Evan said irritably when the darkness had swallowed Violet up, 'It seems we're a constant source of interest to the family—rather, some people who live here.'

Meredith put out a hand and touched his arm. 'Don't be cross,' she murmured. 'They're very sweet, really.'

'You mean Violet and my grandmother are in cahoots?'

'*And* Mrs Whittington. They were very worried that you might take ... exception to my being here or vice versa.'

'My God,' he marvelled a little bitterly, then he put his hand on hers and started to grin reluctantly. 'Well,' he said after some thought, 'let's put their minds totally at rest, shall we? Just in case we have any more unseen spectators.' And before she realised what he was about, he leant across and kissed her forehead. 'I'm very happy to have you back, Merry,' he said quite loudly. 'And very pleased to hear of your successes. I hope we'll be seeing a lot more of you, my dear.' He released her hand and looked at her expectantly.

She cleared her throat and silently commanded her inner tears to cease. 'I'm very glad to be back, Evan,' she said surprisingly steadily. 'Thank you. And, incidentally, I think it would be a great idea to put Nuriootpa in foal.'

Not much later, though, that silent welling of tears in her heart that had come so suddenly on top of laughter found release, and she wept into her pillow.

For what? she asked herself torturedly. You knew it was over. *You* ended it yourself, didn't you? Were you foolish enough in your heart of hearts, Meredith, to hope that Evan would find he couldn't live without you? Well, he can, he showed that tonight quite clearly. It's *over* for him, finished, dead. Oh *God* ...

Chris arrived early the next morning, laden down with birthday gifts, one of them of a most improbable nature.

'A ... a ... computer?' Mrs Sommerville said dazedly.

'Do I need one?'

'Every household should have one, especially one this size,' Chris declared. 'For your accounts—oh, just for fun if need be.'

'But I have absolutely *no* idea how they work!'

'I'll teach you, Gran.'

'Darling—dear Chris, I'm *eighty-two* today!'

'So what? Now if I tried to tell you you were getting senile and . . .'

'I am not! Well . . .'

'There you go, dear, darling Grandmama,' Chris said affectionately. 'I promise you, you'll have a lot of fun with this little baby. Just you wait and see.' And indeed, his grandmother couldn't hide the sudden spark of speculation and intrigue in her eyes as she gazed at the present.

Chris smiled around smugly at everyone else, then a sudden rush of the enthusiasm with which he had greeted Meredith overcame him again and he said, 'On a similar subject—of dearness anyway—darling Merry, I'm so delighted to see you! When are you going to invite me up to Townsville to view your empire?'

'Any time you care to come, Chris, but it's no empire.'

'Ah, but we Sommervilles have the golden touch, don't we? I'm very glad you've forgiven me, by the way,' he added, drawing her out of earshot of everyone else. 'Evan was surprisingly forgiving too, you know.'

'Was he? I'm glad,' she said, and he eyed her curiously. 'Now, Chris,' she said after a moment, 'don't . . .'

'I'm not, I won't,' he promised. 'I mean I won't go around rushing in where angels fear to tread, but . . .'

'Chris,' it was Meredith's turn to break in, which she did with a distinctly warning note in her voice, 'I'll never forgive you again, I promise.'

'Oh, all right,' he conceded ruefully. 'But—well, never mind! I've banished the thought,' he added hastily. 'How long are you staying?'

'Until tomorrow.'

It wasn't until after lunch that Meredith found time to go down to the stables. A lot of the district people and employees popped in to wish Mrs Sommerville well and they were regaled with birthday cake and sherry, although the formal, family party with another specially iced cake was planned for afternoon tea. In fact, after lunch, an air of lethargy seemed to grip Sommerville and Mrs Sommerville herself went to bed for a nap.

'Why don't you take a rest, Meredith?' she suggested.

'No, I'm fine, thank you, Mrs Sommerville. And anyway I haven't seen Nuriootpa yet. I also thought I should have a look at the winery—I've never really done that since it's been in operation again. And—well, I'm afraid I won't have time tomorrow.'

'It's very interesting, the winery,' said Violet. 'I could spend hours in there.'

'It is,' Mrs Sommerville agreed, but with a sigh. 'I wish you didn't have to go back so soon, my dear,' she said.

'So do I. But I promise you it won't be so long before I come to see you again. Actually, I was thinking too that when winter comes—the winters are lovely in Towns-ville—you might like to come up and see me? You and Violet.'

Mrs Sommerville brightened. 'What a grand idea,' she said slowly. 'Why on earth shouldn't I? I mean, if I can learn to work a computer what's to stop me hopping on an aeroplane? Don't you agree, Violet?'

'Always wanted to see Townsville, actually,' Violet said.

When Meredith arrived at the stables, there was no one about, so she was able to have a tearful reunion with Nuriootpa, although a stable-hand did appear in time to help her saddle up the mare. But she saw no one else as she and Nuriootpa walked through the blindingly hot, still, white afternoon.

'I hope it rains soon,' she said to the mare, as she realised how dry Sommerville was. 'Had you thought of having a baby, by the way? Evan thinks it would be a good idea. So do I, I'm sure you'd have lovely foals.'

But she didn't go for a long ride, it was too hot, and she handed the mare back to the same stable-hand, still the only person about, apparently.

'Awful hot, isn't is, Mrs Meredith?' he said genially.

'It certainly is! How long since you've had rain?'

'A good while, but I reckon it won't be much longer. In fact I wouldn't be 't-all surprised if we get a proper storm this afternoon. It's right muggy.'

'I just hope it doesn't wash any vines away this time,' Meredith said. 'Which reminds me, I was going to take a look at the winery.'

'Not a bad spot to be, ma'am. It's nice and cool in there. If I were you I'd do just that.'

'I will.'

But she didn't. She gave Nuriootpa a last pat and wandered away in that direction, looking idly into all the boxes as she went. And she saluted Nhulunbuy and Nunawadding and turned the corner out of sight of the washbays and Nuriootpa's box.

The stable complex was L-shaped with the short end of the L going up towards the winery. But at the last box, she hesitated. It was empty and had obviously been recently cleaned and laid down with new, sweet-smelling straw. It was also dim inside and cool-looking, and she glanced away towards the winery, with its white walls and gables shimmering a little in the heat, and she thought, no, I don't really want to go in there. It will remind me of Sarah and everything I don't want to think about any more, can't bear to think about.

And without thinking much more about it, she stepped into the empty box and sat down on the straw staring at her hands. Then she sighed and laid her head back against the brick wall and felt the sweat run down behind her ears and between her breasts. She closed her eyes, gripped at last by the lethargy that had kept most other, more sensible, mortals on Sommerville indoors.

She fell asleep.

She had no idea what woke her or how long she had slept, but she came awake with a pounding heart, for something had wrenched her from sleep, curled up in the straw, to being wide awake and sitting up apprehensively.

She blinked and realised that it had gone dark outside, but a curious sort of darkness, like an eclipse of the sun she remembered from her childhood, and a glance at her watch confirmed that it was only three-thirty. She started to scramble up—and then heard a tumult of voices and a whooshing sort of roar that for several moments paralysed her with fright.

Then she sniffed and her eyes widened in sudden comprehension.

The scene that met her as she stumbled out of the box was terrifying. The winery roof was ablaze and people were running everywhere manning extinguishers and pumping furiously at the water-cart which was always kept full in case of just such an emrgency. But as the puny-looking jet of water finally made roof level, half of the roof collapsed inwards with a horrible crash.

Meredith found herself clinging to the box door, for a breeze was blowing the black smoke towards her and she couldn't really make out the figures round the winery. Heavy black clouds above had also diminished the daylight and there was lightning flickering.

She was not to know until later that she had slept through the first bolt of lightning and crack of thunder, the bolt which had scored a direct hit on the old thatch of the winery roof and set it alight, that it was another crack of thunder that had woken her, by which time the roof was well ablaze.

All she knew as she peered through the haze of smoke was a terrible sense of fear.

Then she heard Evan shouting. 'It's too late, we can't save the roof—just concentrate on the walls and the grass around it. Are we *sure* everyone is out? Do a double head count.'

'I'm quite sure, Mr Sommerville,' a strange voice answered, and Meredith felt her chest muscles loosen.

Then another voice called. 'What about Mrs Meredith? She said she was going up there.' It was the stable-hand who had taken Nuriootpa from her.

'I'm here,' she tried to call. 'It's all right, I'm here!' But her voice didn't seem to carry. Not nearly as well as Violet's—Meredith discovered she could see her bulky figure and realised that the wind had shifted—and she started to run as she heard Violet saying, 'She's not up at the house. And she did say she was going to visit . . .'

'*No!* Evan, no!' Chris yelled then as Meredith tripped in her haste and fell. 'Hang on, the rest of the roof is going to go any minute. Let's *think*. For God's sake, Evan, you can't go in there with no protection, nothing . . .'

'I'm here—oh, please, I'm here!' Meredith screamed, getting her voice going at last, as she got up on to her knees.

Everyone swung round, Evan included, in mid-stride only feet away from the winery doorway and there was an unnatural silence for a couple of moments.

Then Evan was covering the ground towards her with even longer strides and when he got to her, he swept her to her feet and into his arms, burying his smoke-blackened face in her hair and holding her as if he would never let her go, so hard that she could feel his heart beating against her breast, with heavy, slamming strokes—of fear.

Then the rest of the roof crashed in, but he didn't even look back over his shoulder. He just picked her up and walked away with her, down the path she had come up from the stables, and by some curious instinct perhaps, into that last, empty box, where no one could see them.

He staggered then and she clutched at him fearfully, but he lowered himself carefully to the straw with her in his lap, and rocked backwards and forwards, still holding her as close as he could and saying her name over and over into her hair.

It was an age before she felt him begin to relax at last, to be still at last, and finally to begin to release her.

'*Don't*,' she whispered convulsively, and clutched at him again.

But he held her away and managed to smile exhaustedly down at her. 'I must. Sorry about that. I . . . it . . . I got carried away in the heat of the moment. It won't happen again.'

She stared up at him and her eyes filled with tears. 'But I want it to,' she said hoarsely and fearfully. 'Don't you understand? I didn't know you felt like that—I thought it was only me. I thought you'd got over me and I felt like dying. I—I didn't know that you really *cared*,' her voice sank, 'like that. But perhaps I've got it wrong again . . . Oh God.' And she turned her face into his shoulder and started to cry despairingly.

'Merry, don't.' Evan stroked her hair. 'Please! It's not that.' He waited a while, then tilted her chin so that she had to look at him. And he smudged her tears with his fingers, leaving black marks on her cheeks.

'What is it, then?' she managed to whisper at last as her body still shuddered in his arms.

He closed his eyes and rested his head back against the wall. 'It's not that I don't love you. It's always been the opposite, if anything—I love you too much. I told you once that from the moment I saw you standing in the moonlight, I was struck. But that was probably the understatement of all time, because it was so much more. So that not to be able to possess you and make you love me in return was . . . was like a constant, burning brand within me. To imagine my brother Leigh possessing you was an indescribable torment—to imagine *any* other man was the same. Not to know why you'd done what you did that first night, to think that it might have just been a . . . a kiss in time for you, was the same. Merry, loving you has made some kind of a monster out of me, and I never realised it so clearly as when you said, on Dunk, that you thought I could even have gone so far as to marry Sarah to punish you.'

'Well, I could have,' he said in a voice drained of all emotion. 'Not consciously or coherently, but the urge was there. So many things . . . I couldn't even bear the thought of you making love to me the way you might have with Leigh. I had to make it something new for you, something . . .'

'You did, you did,' she wept. 'I tried to tell you—show you, but I did want . . .' She stopped.

'What did you want?' he asked gently, opening his eyes at last and looking down at her.

'I wanted it to be *us* making love, not you making love to me. That was one of the reasons why I thought you didn't really love me, that you couldn't forgive me.'

He sighed. 'What is there to forgive? That you didn't fall in love with me on the spot, the way I did?' His lips twisted. 'If anyone had told me it could happen to me like that—like the lightning that struck the winery roof—I'd never have believed them, so you see . . .'

'No. No, Evan it . . . you . . .'

'Mr Sommerville?' Violet's voice called from outside, causing them both to jump.

Then Evan gritted his teeth but managed to say astonishingly politely, 'Violet, will you do me a favour? Will you go away? She's quite all right and I'm not hurting her—for once,' he added barely audibly.

'Oh,' said Violet, unseen. 'Okay. But I just thought you'd like to know the fire is out. It didn't spread.'

'That's splendid news, Violet, thank you. Now will you . . .'

'I'm going,' Violet said hastily, and could be heard departing up the path.

'That woman won't be happy until she drives me round the bend,' Evan remarked bitterly. 'Merry . . .'

'Evan,' Meredith whispered, 'you're wrong. You are hurting me. If you send me away now, I'll be hurt until the day I die. Please give me a chance to say . . . I've never been able to find the right words or the right time to . . .' her voice shook, 'to tell you how it was for me. It was never just a kiss in time for me. If it had been, I could never have felt so stunned and shocked, and not known what to think of myself. But, if you've any idea what it's like to belong to a man, even if he doesn't want you, and suddenly begin to understand that anything you ever felt for him might not have been ... been worth the paper it was written on compared to a small space in time and another man. Can you *ever* understand,' she said anguishedly, 'that to be released from a mistake like that—the way I was—doesn't diminish it but if anything magnifies it? But none of that torture changed the way I felt about you. Nothing, not even all my self-mockery could alter something deep inside me that seemed to be irrevocably committed to you. Something that started that night. You said ... you said once that we had always wanted each other. But do you really think that want could have survived these awful years if it hadn't been something more? You,' her eyes sparkled with tears, 'you proved that to me just now. Tell me what *I* have to do to prove it to *you*, because if you do send me away now I'll know that you can't trust me even if you love me.'

He made a husky sound in his throat and drew her close. 'Merry, that's exactly what I'm trying to make you understand. If I could have ever been rational about it, I'd have known that Leigh must have rushed you off your feet into an unsuitable marriage, I'd have been able to work it out. But did I do that? Oh no.' He held her even closer with a naked kind of savagery.

'Evan,' her voice was muffled against his shirt, 'it was my fault that you didn't know all of it. I've made as many mistakes ...'

He held her away abruptly. 'Chris didn't believe what I believed of you. Gran wouldn't have if she'd known—she would have simply refused to believe it from her knowledge of you. But what did I do? I immediately believed the worst of you. And even when I could no longer believe that, I still couldn't bear to think of you having had anything to do with Leigh. Merry, there's something about you that ... *moves* me so much I ... I just can't explain it. Except to say that I love you far too much ever to be any good for you. Do you really want a jealous, suspicious, possessive—*irrational* husband?'

'What I want,' she said softly, and knew in her heart that he would probably be all of those things from time to time throughout their life, just as she knew now that there was an invisible cord that bound her to Evan Sommerville, and him to her, that could never be severed, 'is a husband who will at least let me prove to him how much I love him.' She raised trembling fingers to his face. 'Please,' she whispered.

'Merry.'

'Er ... Evan?' It was Chris this time whose voice made them jump.

Evan took a deep breath and said menacingly, '*Chris!*'

'Evan, believe me,' Chris broke in, 'not for the world would I normally want to ... er ... interrupt you, but it is rather important, I'm afraid. You see,' he continued hurriedly, 'one of the main winery walls is very unstable now and it looks as if it could collapse. I *thought* it might be wise to give it a hand with the front-end loader before it falls down on top of someone, but ...'

'Then why don't you!' Evan demanded.

'Well,' Chris hesitated, 'I don't quite like to take upon myself the task of more or less totally demolishing the place. It is an historic building in a sense and the place is your pride and joy, after all. And I did think you might be able to come up with another solution, so ...'

'Chris, right at this moment, I would be totally happy if

you went ahead and totally demolished Sommerville and some of the people who inhabit it! Just do it.'

'It might need a total rebuild, Evan . . .'

'Chris!'

'I'm going, I'm going,' Chris said hastily. 'Er . . . give my love to Merry.'

Evan made a convulsive movement, but Meredith slid her arms around his neck and smiled into his shoulder. And after a moment she felt the tension drain out of him and he said very quietly, 'My pride and joy? More like my folly. I only ever took up wine-making as an excuse to come back to Sommerville to live. To be close to you. Yet almost the first thing I did was terrorise you into leaving.'

'I didn't take my heart with me,' she murmured. 'If you hadn't found me first, I'd have come back.'

'Merry,' he said presently, 'unfortunately, I don't think my intentions are proof against this kind of proximity for much longer.' His lips curved into a wry smile, but his eyes were deadly serious and watchful. 'If you had any sense, you'd get up and run a mile now, my darling.'

'I am going to get up,' she said very softly, and felt him tense so she held him and pressed her cheek into his shoulder, 'but only to do this.'

She extricated herself slowly then and got up, and he didn't move, but his eyes never left her as she stepped over to the door and pulled both halves firmly closed.

Then she came back and knelt down in the straw in front of him.

'Do you think that will deter them?' Evan asked a little unsteadily.

'For the time being.' She smiled at him. 'They'll be very busy pushing down walls.' She reached for his hand which was grazed as well as black and raised it to her lips and kissed it lingeringly, then placed it over her heart. Then she said shakily, 'I'm still not very good at running.'

His fingers moved on her body beneath hers and then with a groan he gathered her back into his arms.

They made love right there on the bed of straw, oblivious to all that was going on around them. Meredith didn't even hear the winery wall collapse into a heap of rubble, or the rain which finally came. She heard nothing but the things Evan said to her so huskily that they might have been torn right from his most inner being, words of love. She didn't feel the straw beneath her, only his weight upon her and his heart beating heavily again as he took her with an urgency that told of a sense of need so great it was impossible to control. And she loved him in return, not only with her body but the very depths of her soul.

They lay in each other's arms afterwards with their bodies still entwined. The feeble light of a sunset struggling to break through the clouds came through the one small, high window and laid a luminous sheen on their bare limbs.

Evan moved at last, but only to pillow his head on her breasts, and she brought up a hand to stroke his hair. Then he rolled away from her and pushed himself up on one elbow to gaze down at her. 'All right?' he asked gently. 'I didn't hurt you? I've always been afraid I—might.'

'No, you never have. I love you,' she added, smiling up at him with tears sparkling in her eyes, 'so very much.'

He bent his head to kiss her eyelids, then slid his arms around her and cradled her to him so tenderly, she could have died at the wonder of it.

A lot later he said with an effort, 'What—what do you think is going on outside?'

A faint smile curved her lips. 'I don't know. It sounds awfully quiet.'

'Mmm,' he agreed, and kissed the curve of her shoulder. 'Too quiet. Do you know what I wish? That I could spirit you away from here without having to encounter any of . . . *our* relations or anyone else. I've got the horrible feeling they're up there planning a reception committee for us.'

'You could,' Meredith whispered. 'Tomorrow, anyway. You could come up to Townsville with me and help me to sort out my affairs.'

'What a brilliant idea,' he murmured. 'Just one thing. Your friend up there.'

'Laura?'

'Yes. Does she take as obsessive an interest in you as everyone here does?'

'Well,' a spark of mischief glinted in Meredith's eyes, but she went on hastily at the look of serious misgiving he cast her, 'no, not really. No, she doesn't.'

'Thank God,' he said wryly. 'In that case, should we go up and put them out of their misery? Just in case they come looking for us again.'

'Oh, definitely!' She laughed up at him.

Evan caught his breath and hugged her to him.

Harlequin Presents

Coming Next Month

Available in January wherever paperback books are sold, or through Harlequin Reader Service:

In the U.S.
901 Fuhrmann Blvd.
P.O. Box 1397
Buffalo, N.Y. 14240-1397

In Canada
P.O. Box 603
Fort Erie, Ontario
L2A 5X3

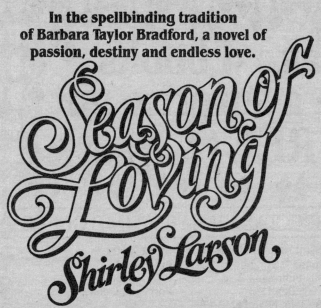
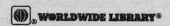

Take 4 books & a surprise gift FREE

SPECIAL LIMITED-TIME OFFER

Mail to   **Harlequin Reader Service®**

In the U.S.   In Canada
901 Fuhrmann Blvd.   P.O. Box 609
P.O. Box 1394   Fort Erie, Ontario
Buffalo, N.Y. 14240-1394   L2A 5X3

YES! Please send me 4 free Harlequin Romance® novels
and my free surprise gift. Then send me 8 brand-new novels every
month as they come off the presses. Bill me at the low price of
$1.99 each*—an 11% saving off the retail price. There are no
shipping, handling or other hidden costs. There is no minimum
number of books I must purchase. I can always return a shipment
and cancel at any time. Even if I never buy another book from
Harlequin, the 4 free novels and the surprise gift are mine to keep
forever.   118 BPR BP7F

*Plus 89¢ postage and handling per shipment in Canada.

Name   (PLEASE PRINT)

Address   Apt. No.

City   State/Prov.   Zip/Postal Code

This offer is limited to one order per household and not valid to present
subscribers. Price is subject to change.   DOR-SUB-1D

Readers rave about Harlequin American Romance!

" ...the best series of modern romances
 I have read...great, exciting, stupendous,
 wonderful."
> –S.E.,* Coweta, Oklahoma

" ...they are absolutely fantastic...going to be
 a smash hit and hard to keep on the
 bookshelves."
> –P.D., Easton, Pennsylvania

" The American line is great. I've enjoyed
 every one I've read so far."
> –W.M.K., Lansing, Illinois

" ...the best stories I have read in a long
 time."
> –R.H., Northport, New York

*Names available on request.